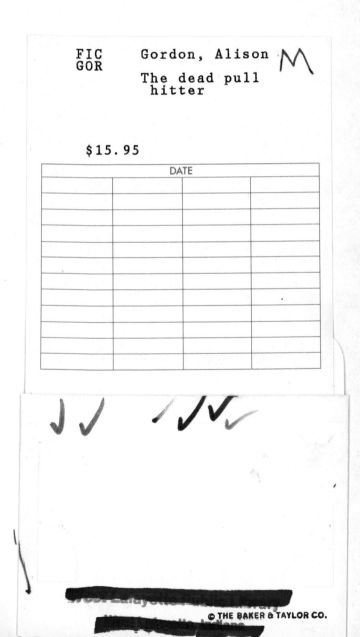

FIC   Gordon, Alison M
GOR

The dead pull
   hitter

$15.95

DATE			

THE DEAD PULL HITTER

ALISON GORDON

THE DEAD PULL HITTER

St. Martin's Press
New York

Thanks are due to Charis Wahl, Charles Gordon, and
Larry Humber

The content and characters in this book are fiction.
Any resemblance to actual persons or happenings is coincidental.

10 |89 BₐT 9·57

Library of Congress Cataloging-in-Publication Data

Gordon, Alison.
        The dead pull hitter / Alison Gordon.
                p.   cm.
        ISBN 0-312-03319-2
        I. Title.
    PR9199.3.G617D4   1989
    813'.54—dc20   89-34862
                                                                  CIP

First published in Canada by McClelland and Stewart.

First U.S. Edition

10 9 8 7 6 5 4 3 2 1

For Isaac Anderson and King Gordon for their love of words and Paul Bennett for his words of love.

The reading light over my seat didn't work. It had been burned out the last time I was on the plane, so I shouldn't have been surprised. I moved to the aisle seat, the one with the non-reclining chair back, strapped myself in, and opened my book.

I was already in a bad mood. We had been sitting on the ground at LaGuardia Airport for half an hour. The equipment truck had a flat tire, and we couldn't leave until it got there. The passengers in the rows behind me were socking back drinks and getting more unruly by the minute. I wanted a cigarette badly.

Claire, the purser, leaned across me and lowered the tray table on the window seat. She set down a couple of baby bottles of vodka, a can of tonic, and a glass of ice.

"You look as though you could use this."

"You are an angel. How much longer?"

"The truck just got here," she said. "The way the guys are going, I hope they load fast. It's getting pretty drunk out."

"Tell me about it," I said.

The guys she referred to were the Toronto Titans baseball team, currently in first place in the American League East. They had just swept the Yankees in New York and our charter flight was headed to Toronto for the last home stand of the season. They were more cocky and arrogant than usual. And that's going some.

"Yo, Hank! What kind of shit did you write tonight?"

Stinger Swain, the third baseman, yelled at me from his seat five rows back, a mean little smirk on his sallow face. He had just folded his poker hand and was looking for other sport. I tried to ignore him.

"Yo, Lady Writer! I'm talking to you," he said, tossing his empty beer can at me. "Did you write about your hero Preacher's catch in the eighth inning? If my white ass looked as good as his black one in uniform, would you write about me all the time, too?"

And kids lined up for this guy's autograph? I turned in my seat.

"I wrote about you today, Stinger."

"The lady's finally learning to appreciate the finer points of the game."

"I wrote about the way you looked sliding into third: like a pregnant seal trying to climb an ice floe."

That earned me a few appreciative hoots. Alejandro Jones, the second baseman, barked and slapped his palms together like flippers.

"Shut up, Taco-breath," Swain said, then turned to Goober Grabowski, his seatmate. "Deal the cards."

We finally took off, to the accompaniment of sarcastic cheers and vulgar noises. As the no-smoking sign clicked off, Moose Greer, the team public relations director, dropped his seat back in the row in front of me and peered at me through the gap.

"Glad to be going home?"

"It's been a long road trip."

And a long season. I had spent just about enough time on the Flying Fart, which was what the clever fellows behind me call this elderly bird, for reasons I won't go into. Trust me, the name is appropriate.

Because of the one a.m. jet curfew at Pearson International, and, I suspect, the high pockets of Titan owner Ted Ferguson, we fly a propeller-driven plane after night games. It's the airborne equivalent of the spring-shot buses that at one time or another transported most of this same gang through the minor leagues – reliable, but not luxurious. The seats are covered in faded orange and green, clashing horribly with the sky-blue-and-red pop art patterns on the bulkheads. But we ride in relative comfort, with a friendly crew and plenty of food and booze.

It's a funny little world on the airplane, a society in which each member knows his, or her, own place. Literally. The seating never varies.

Red O'Brien, the manager, sits alone in the right front row of seats. The travelling secretary has the left side. Coaches take the next two rows and the trainer, his assistant, the equipment manager, and Moose Greer are just behind.

The writers and broadcasters sit in the next couple of rows and the players have the rest of the plane: the Bible readers and sleepers towards the front; the cardplayers and drinkers next; and the rookies in the very back. I am the only woman on board who doesn't serve drinks.

I'm Katherine Henry. My friends call me Kate. I am a baseball writer by trade, and for the past five years I've spent the best months of Toronto's calendar everywhere but at home, following the Titans all over the American League map.

I'm forty, older than most of the Titans, including the manager. I'm tallish, prettyish, and a lot more interesting than most of the people I write about, but I love baseball. On the really good days I can't believe I'm paid to do my job.

I'm also good at it, to the active disappointment of some of my male colleagues, who have been waiting for me to fall flat since the day I walked into my first spring training. By now I have earned some grudging respect.

So has the team. They have never finished higher than fourth in the tough Eastern Division in the ten years they've been a team, but this season they began winning in spring training and forgot to stop. They slipped into first place in the beginning of June and have been there ever since.

There are a number of reasons for this. Stinger Swain is one. He's having a career season, with a batting average well over .300 and 37 home runs going into the last week of the season. But he isn't the only one. Red likes to say that if they award a new car for the Most Valuable Player this year they should make it a bus. Managers always like to say that. They find it in the media phrase book they get at manager school. It's right in there with "He pitched well enough to win," "We're just taking it one game at a time," and "You can't win any ballgames if you don't score any runs."

But Stinger is this year's star, unfortunately for the writers. Swain is a singularly unpleasant person, a vulgar, racist, sexist bully who embodies everything wrong with a society that finds its heroes on playing fields. He delights in making the writers uncomfortable. In my case, he insists upon doing all interviews in the nude. And his hands are never idle.

But there are more pleasant players. The best story of the year is Mark Griffin, an engaging lefthanded rookie reliever with 20 saves. He's just twenty-one, a real pheenom, and a Canadian, born and raised in my neighbourhood. They call him "Archie," because he's got red hair, freckles, and went to Riverdale Collegiate. His best buddy on the team is another lefthander, Flakey Patterson. When he and Griffin became friends, some of the players started calling Flakey Jughead. Swain and Grabowski called him Veronica.

Griffin is relatively sane, but Patterson is a Central Casting lefthanded pitcher – loony as a tune. During the three years he has been with the Titans, he's tried meditation, EST, self-hypnotism, macrobiotics, tai chi, and Norman Vincent Peale, and he alternates periods of extreme self-denial with bouts of excess. During the All-Star break, in protest over not being chosen for the team, he dyed his hair bright orange and wore it clipped close on the sides and long on top: as close to punk as is possible in the conservative world of sport.

He is the third starter in the rotation. The first, the Titans' erstwhile ace, is righthander Steve Thorson, Stevie the K, a twelve-year veteran and winner of a couple of Cy Young awards when he pitched for the Dodgers. His handsome blue-eyed face and body that won't quit are used to sell everything from breakfast cereal to men's cologne. He's mobbed for autographs wherever he goes. Grown men and women pack giant K's in their ballpark bags to wave when he strikes a batter out. He's the biggest star the Titans have ever had. And he's an insufferable prick.

The television guys love him, because he's always glad to see them. It might have something to do with the money they slip him for interviews, but I think it's also a matter of control. They only want thirty-second clips and feed him soft questions. He can do without the print guys. It's not that he refuses to talk to us, he just talks such self-serving crap that I hate to write it down.

He's not popular with the team, either. He always

finds a way to blame his failure on others. The centre fielder or second baseman should have caught the ball that fell in for a game-winning hit. The catcher called for the wrong pitch. The manager shouldn't have taken him out of the game when he did, or, sometimes, should have when he didn't.

But he's a winner, which counts for a lot. Or he was until this season. Either age or opposing hitters caught up with him, and the former 20-game winner had only 13 going into the last week of the season.

It's ironic that the season they might win it all has been his worst, but I'm secretly delighted. His role as a winner was taken over by Tony Costello, nicknamed Bony because he's not, a lefthander with his own set of idiosyncrasies. He's a lunchbucket kind of guy from New Jersey, simple and matter-of-fact, but a total neurotic, so wrapped up in his phobias he has trouble functioning. He's afraid of flying, heights, the dark, germs, snakes, insects, and, most of all, failure. This last despite the fact that he's having a dream season. With 21 wins, he's a contender for the Cy Young Award, carrying the team on his pudgy shoulders. That scares him, too.

I looked back to where he was sitting, just behind Swain. He clutched a drink in one hand and a cigarette in the other, staring straight ahead. There were eight little Scotch bottles lined up on his tray. A typical trip for Bony. He's a candidate for the detox centre after a trip to the coast.

This road trip had been rough: Chicago, Detroit, and New York, all towns in which a person could get into a lot of trouble if she were so inclined. This late in the season I was so inclined I was almost bent. I was looking forward to a long night in my own bed.

I undid my seat belt and headed back towards the john, excusing myself past the players in the aisles. A few pretended not to hear me or refused to move, then made lewd remarks as I squeezed past. Steve Thorson yelled something about the back of the plane being off limits to the press. What a bunch of jokers, eh? Some fun.

The smiling face of Tiny Washington was a beacon. Surely the sweetest man on the team, he never gave me a hard time.

"The lovely Kate Henry," he murmured as I got to his seat, his voice a rich bass. "It's always a pleasure to see you. You're always welcome in my part of the world."

"Cut the crap, Tiny," I said. He winked.

"Stop by for visit on your way back. We'll have us a little conversation."

Washington was one of the most sophisticated players on the team, but he hid it well. If people wanted to think he was nothing but a slow, friendly, shuck-and-jive kind of guy from the ghetto in Washington, D.C., that was fine with him. It made his life a lot easier. But I was lucky enough to find out early on what was behind the facade. It had made my life a lot easier.

That first spring, Tiny came up to me by the batting cage after a few days, introduced himself, offered to answer any questions I might have, then left me alone. I took him at his word and used him as a sounding board for my early perceptions.

It wasn't characteristic of him. He usually let reporters come to him. At the end of the season he explained why, late one night in the hotel bar in Cleveland.

"I watched the other writers and the way they were treating you. I listened to the other players. I could see how scared you were, but more important, I could see that you had pride. I thought maybe someone should give you a chance."

Then he had sensed how moved I was, finished his drink, and moved on.

"Hey, I give all the rookies a hand, if they know how to take it," he said. "You knew how."

That season, Tiny was the only legitimate star the team had. He was a veteran, admired by players all over the league. He set an example for the young Titans, especially the blacks, and smoothed my way with a word here and there to players on other teams. It helped a lot, and I was grateful.

Now he was at the end of his career, and smart enough to know it. He might have a few years left as a designated hitter, but there was a young player ready to take his place at first base. Hal Cooper, a.k.a. Kid, was a big farm boy from Nebraska who had been biding his time in Triple A for the last couple of years. He was called up when the rosters increased in September and Tiny had gone out of his way to help him. I hoped the Kid knew how to take the hand, too.

2

I ran the water into the toy sink until it was cold, then splashed it on my face. I felt grubby and looked like hell in the dim cold neon light. I'd lost the battle for control of my curly red hair, and the dark circles under my eyes weren't wayward mascara. I did the best I could with lipstick and hairbrush and went back out.

And walked straight into a fight.

Steve Thorson was halfway out of his seat, talking angrily to Joe Kelsey, the left fielder, who was standing in the aisle.

"What are you worrying about the pitchers for, Preacher? You just concentrate on catching routine fly balls and I'll do my job."

"How do you catch a fly ball when it lands in the upper deck, Thorson? That's where yours are going lately."

"Go read your Bible. I've got better things to do than talk to some asshole with all his brains in his bat. Or read some scouting reports, for a change, if your lips aren't too tired. The Bible doesn't tell you how to play left field."

Kelsey started towards Thorson, but Tiny Washington moved between them.

"You got a big mouth, Thorson," he said, "and a short memory. Seems like you only remember games we lost. I do believe that the Preacher has won one or two for you over the years. So why don't you go back to sucking on your beer and leave the man alone."

Thorson settled back in his seat warily. Not many players stood up to Tiny Washington when he stopped kidding around. When he was angry, it was best to keep out of his way.

Looking around him, Tiny realized that he had an audience.

"Seems like there are too many people on this team thinking about themselves," he growled. "All's we got to do is win four more games, but some folks think it's time to start fighting each other. How 'bout we save it for the Red Sox."

As he walked back to his seat in the sudden silence, the others squirmed like Sunday school kids caught stealing from the poor box. He smiled at me and motioned me into the middle seat in his row, next to Eddie Carter, the right fielder.

"You don't want to go making something big out of this, now. They're just kids. The pressure is getting to them."

"Thorson's no kid, Tiny. He's been through the pressure before."

"He's no kid, but he's stupid sometimes. Preacher shouldn't have listened to him."

"Preacher was right," said Carter, Kelsey's best friend. "Thorson's always blaming everything on us."

"Yeah, but anybody that knows anything knows that Thorson is full of shit. Excuse me, Kate."

Tiny's old-fashioned courtliness always tickles me. He should hang around the newsroom sometime. The language is worse there than in any locker room I've visited.

"So what do you think, Tiny? Are you guys going to win the pennant?"

"Sweeping the Yankees in their park was big. Even if they win the next nine games, all we have to win is four. At home. Looks like a lock to me."

"But what about the fat lady? It's not over until she sings."

"I do believe I can hear her warming up."

Carter chimed in with a falsetto hum, and we all laughed.

"Seriously, Tiny. People in Toronto are used to losing. They're just waiting to see you blow it the way the Maple Leafs and the Argos do every year."

"Well, you just write in your column that Tiny says not to worry. We'll have the whole thing wrapped up by the end of the weekend."

"Yeah? You're playing the Red Sox and the Yankees are playing Cleveland. You can't count on the Indians to help you."

"Then we'll just have to help ourselves."

"Okay, fine. I'll pass on your inspirational message to my faithful readers. You just keep your guys in line and get it over with."

I went back to the front of the plane. As I strapped myself back into my seat, Bill Sanderson, the *World* reporter, looked up from the book of statistics on his food tray.

"What's happening back there?"

"Nothing," I lied, opening my book.

Terminal One was deserted when we landed at one-thirty. The whole planeload trudged, some stumbling a bit, through the long corridors to the immigration desks. I found the line with the fewest Latin American players in it. If anyone was going to get held up it would be one of them. I was behind Archie Griffin. He greeted me warmly. He hadn't been around long enough to know that he was supposed to hate reporters.

"Hi, Archie. Nice game tonight."

He looked a bit embarrassed, and maybe a tad tipsy.

"Can I ask a favour, Kate? It's personal."

"Why not?"

"Could you stop calling me Archie? I hate that name."

"We've been calling you Archie all year. Why didn't you say something?"

"I'm a rookie. What could I say?"

"The season you've had, they should call you anything you want, Mark."

He smiled, a little sheepishly.

"Thanks. It's really been getting to my mum. Mark was my dad's name."

His father had died when Griffin was nine. His mother was a professor of medieval history at the University of Toronto who didn't know what to make of the alien being she had created.

"How is your mum? Enjoying the pennant race?"

"You wouldn't believe it, but she is. She even rented a TV."

"Amazing. You're up."

Griffin turned and went to the immigration desk. It didn't take him long to be passed through. I had my citizenship card out, gave it to the inspector, told her I had nothing to declare, and was handed a card with a code scrawled across the top, describing me, I hoped, as an upstanding citizen.

I met Gloves Gardiner on the escalator to the baggage claim. Just the man I wanted to see.

"What was that all about between Preacher and Thorson?"

"Sir Stephen's got his shorts in a knot and Preacher was handy."

"What's his problem now?"

"He's in a fight with his agent."

"Sam Craven? I thought he fired him."

"So did Steve. But there's still six months to run on their contract and Craven's not going to stand aside. He's threatening to sue."

"I don't blame him. Thorson's Titan contract is up for renewal and his agent's cut will be a nice little taste."

"You got it. Craven showed up at the stadium before the game tonight. Before you got there."

I'd missed the team bus, distracted by a late lunch with an old flame during which we had challenged the Aquavit supply of a Danish restaurant near his office. The players who had noticed I missed the bus were giving me a hard time about it.

"What happened?"

"Some shouting in the clubhouse."

"Were any of the other writers around?"

"No."

"Thanks for the tip."

"You didn't hear it from me."

"Hear what?"

Gloves was my spy. A man with a strong iconoclastic bent, he had taken a liking to me as soon as he saw how much some of the other reporters and players disapproved.

He has been around for dog's years, never a star, but good enough to hang on. He's appreciated not for his hitting or, goodness knows, for his speed on the base-paths, but because he knows how to handle his pitchers: which one needs coaxing, which one needs teasing, and which one needs kicking in the ass. He's aware of how much each had to drink the night before, and after a few warmup pitches he can tell what pitches are working and which aren't, better than the pitcher himself.

He's an odd athlete. He went to college for more than sport. He majored in English and history in the last gasp of the politicized sixties, and he both protested against the Vietnam War and lost his best friend to it.

I leaned against a post by the carousel and yawned. The players were playing baggage roulette, a ritual at the end of a road trip. Flakey Patterson collected a dollar from each player, and the pool went to the guy whose bag appeared first. Preacher Kelsey won it for the second time in a row. He and Eddie Carter exchanged low fives while the others muttered darkly about a fix.

My bag was the third. I grabbed it and humped it past the weary-looking customs agent, who took my card and let me go.

Even at that hour, the waiting area outside was crowded with women and small children, the players' families. The wives were carefully coiffed and made up, most of them dressed to the nines. The kids were cranky.

Until six months ago, I'd had someone waiting for me, too. Mickey used to joke about the recipes he'd exchanged with the other wives and threatened to run away with one of them every time the plane was late.

Mickey worked for the CBC, a nice, solid liberal man who had decided after living with me for three years that he wanted someone waiting for him when he got home. Our parting had been passionless. Now I use an airport limo.

There was a larger group than usual waiting. The booster club was also on hand, sitting off to one side under a crudely painted banner. They were a sweet but sorry collection of misfits wearing Titan hats and tee-shirts. Rodney Hart, the pimply teenager who published their newsletter, called my name. I waved and went the other way, in no mood for statistical analysis at that hour. Besides, he'd probably phone and let me know what he'd found. I could always count on Rodney, bless his heart.

Grumpy drivers waited by half a dozen limos, forced to wait until the last plane landed. That was us, but they wouldn't get any business from the ballplayers. What are wives for? Only those of us on expense accounts were customers.

I passed up the first one on principle. He had an anti-smoking slogan prominently displayed. He was still yelling at me when my driver pulled away from the curb. We both lit up.

He was a wonderful driver. He put on a classical tape and didn't say a word. We glided down the 427 to the QEW, towards the blinking lights on the CN tower. Home.

I was dozing when we turned down my street, floating on music. The canopy of trees, lit by the street lights, had a golden glow. Autumn was coming.

My front porch light was on, a welcoming beacon left by my tenant, Sally Parkes. She shared the ground floor flat with her son. I shared the second and third floors with Elwy.

I heard him as soon as I unlocked the door. A thud off the bed, followed by the heavy patter of paws and guttural meows of inquiry. He came into the living room, saw me, sat down, and began to groom himself.

"Ignoring me again? This is what I get after ten days on the road? Come on, you big fat fraud. Where's my welcome?"

Elwy looked at me, his right front paw poised in

21

front of him. His attempt at injured dignity failed, as usual. He's a twenty-pound neutered tom, with black-and-white markings that give him a silly moustache and droopy pantaloons.

I dropped to my knees and meowed at him, scratching the carpet. He stood up and walked heavily to me, lay down, and rolled over. I scratched his stomach. He closed his eyes and purred, kneading his claws at the air.

Other women have husbands or lovers. I've got Elwy. He's at least as affectionate as most men I know, and a lot less complicated. He's always there when I come home from a road trip, and he never asks any questions or nags me about anything but his next meal.

The reunion over, I checked through my mail. A lot of people wanted money: Ma Bell, Visa, Consumers' Gas, two diseases, two poverties (one Third World and one local), a peace group, a women's shelter, and the New Democratic Party. *Maclean's* offered me a free telephone with my subscription, the National Ballet offered me expensive seats to the series of my choice. A postcard from my sister Sheila on safari in Kenya made me jealous, a letter from my parents made me realize I hadn't called lately, and a note from my dentist reminded me it was checkup time. No money.

I took my suitcase to the bedroom, propped my briefcase on the stairs up to my study, and took off my clothes. I was too tired to brush my teeth.

I pulled a big tee-shirt out of my dresser and rolled into bed without setting the alarm. Just before I fell asleep, Elwy jumped up beside me and curled up under my chin the way he had since he was a kitten. It was ludicrous for a cat his size, but we had adjusted over the years. The last sound I heard was his purring.

3

The first sound I heard the next morning was the god-damned phone. I rolled over, saw it was 8:33, and grabbed the receiver before it could emit another obnoxious warble.

It was Ambrose Callaghan, the assistant sports editor. Who else? He is young, ambitious, and officious beyond the call of his small duty. He is in charge of the sports pages overnight and is incapable of ending his shift without crossing every t and dotting every i on his turnover note for the boss.

Or maybe he just gets lonely. His yearning to reach out and touch is particularly annoying on West Coast road trips, since he's shaky on the concept of time zones. The last time I was in California, he called at six in the morning to ask what days off I planned to take during the next home stand.

"Kate, I've been thinking," he said. Uh oh. "We need a good set-up piece for the Red Sox series. What are you planning to write today?"

"A game story, Ambrose. The series starts tonight.

It's a bit late to set it up for tomorrow's paper. Don't we have the pitching matchups and comparative stats in today?"

"I was thinking in terms of something a bit more psychological. The pressures of the pennant race. There's a lot of interest in the Titans right now. We can use a lot more than you're giving us. The *Mirror*'s got eight pages today."

Aha. It all became clear. The publisher had visited Rosie's desk on his way to the men's room again. He can't tell a line drive from a foul tip, but he knows what sells papers.

"Okay. I'll give it some thought."

"Are you taking any days off? You've got a lot of time owing."

"Gee, Ambrose. With all this space to fill, I don't see how I can do it now."

"But you're up to twenty-three days."

"I'll talk to Jake about it. And thanks for calling. I appreciate the advice. And I think the psychological angle is just the thing. You tell Jake I'll get right on it."

The *Planet* didn't pay all that well, but our union had built in some protection for people like me. Every day I worked over five in a week, the paper owed me a day and a half back. And there are no days off on the road. I could usually accumulate six weeks' paid vacation between the World Series and the winter meetings. I was right on target. Luckily, Jake Watson, my editor, understood this nuance of labour-management relations. Rosie was the only one who ever bugged me.

I thought of going back to sleep, but Elwy had other ideas. He hopped off the bed and stood by the door, meowing.

"Right, Fatso. Breakfast time."

I grabbed my old terrycloth bathrobe, one of Mickey's castoffs. Like me. To Elwy's dismay, I stopped at the bathroom on the way to the kitchen. He expressed his outrage loudly.

"Shut up. You're not starving to death. You could live for two weeks on your stored fat."

I spooned the pinkish guck from a can into his bowl.

"Yum, Seaside Supper/Delices de Mer. Your fave."

He pushed me out of the way and began to gobble. He has a disgusting habit of taking bits of glop out of the bowl and eating them off the floor.

I filled the battered blue kettle and put it on to boil. I heated the teapot and spooned in my own tea mixture – Irish Breakfast with a touch of Earl Grey. Heaven, after ten days of tea brewed from bags in tepid water out of stupid little metal pots. The Americans don't know beans about tea. Or leaves, for that matter. Then I went down to the porch for the papers.

We have three in Toronto: the *World*, which sees itself as the paper of record and is stodgy beyond belief; the *Mirror*, which models itself after the British tabloids, complete with scantily clad bimbos and right-wing views; and my own *Planet*, which occupies the middle ground and often combines the worst features of the other two.

It was good to read Canadian news again. The U.S. papers only notice natural catastrophes or political scandal in Canada. It was nice to read about dull politics and petty crime again. The Liberals were down three points in federal polls, up five provincially. The Tories were in sorry shape in both arenas, and the New Democrats were at a record high. Like the stock market. They'd both probably crash before any good came of it.

Metro Council was debating anti-smoking bylaws and the licensing of cats, the Post Office and Transit Commission were threatening strike, and another wolf had gone missing at the zoo. Business as usual.

I took my tea out into the garden, enjoying the morning warmth. All too soon the ground would be brown and frozen. Sparrows gathered on the telephone wire and yammered at Elwy, who blinked lazily at them from his sunny rock. A pair of blue jays swooped in and landed on a branch of my neighbour's maple, which was starting to turn flame-orange. They peeked down at me, quizzically turning their heads from side to side. It was almost time to put the winter feeders out.

I closed my eyes to smell the lavender and lemon balm and listened to the small natural sounds, glad to be away from screaming sirens and honking horns. The only city sound I could hear was the faint, quaint rumble of a streetcar heading south on Broadview.

Mickey and I bought the house together three years ago. When we split up I bought him out. With the rent my friend Sally pays on the first floor flat I can just about afford the mortgage. Besides, they're like family. Sally takes care of the house and her son T.C. feeds Elwy when I'm away. My real family lives in a small prairie town far enough away that I see them only at Christmas. Sally and I went to university together, but she married right after graduation and moved east when her husband was elected to Parliament, an NDP member. He lost his seat in the next election and they moved to Toronto.

I ran into her at a ballet class shortly after Roger had traded her in on a newer model. The downstairs tenant had just left, so Sally and T.C. moved in. It's worked wonderfully.

Sally is down-to-earth in all her attitudes, a real daughter of the Prairies. But she also has a flakey streak, which comes out most obviously in her clothes. She is a slave to fashion who haunts the second-hand stores and discount houses. She designs and sews clothes, too, and manages to look like tomorrow's fashion pages on a budget as small as her waist.

She recently took a job with a photo gallery on Queen Street West and is seriously into modified punk. On her, it looks great. I tend to buy clothes that are good value only because they last so long. Bargain centres give me claustrophobia. Sales make me glassy-eyed. Every few years I spend enormous amounts of money on a few things that I hope will last me forever. Classic, I call them. Boring, says Sally.

She's also a fabulous mother. T.C. adores her. It's just as well, since his father has selective amnesia when it comes to things like his weekends to take the boy, birthdays, and child support payments.

Sally has always refused to do anything to turn T.C. against his father, but over the years he's figured Roger out on his own. He sees through the excuses. It hurts, but he no longer feels betrayed. He likes his dad fine, but never counts on him.

Sally's vice is matchmaking. She didn't much like Mickey, was overjoyed when he moved out, and has been trying since to set me up with one inappropriate man after another. The latest was a performance artist who worked with bananas and green Jell-O. I told her I'd given up on that the last time I went to a parish supper in my father's church basement.

I left the garden reluctantly. I had a bunch of boring things to do, like laundry and filling out expense sheets. I had just dumped the contents of my suitcase on the bed for sorting when the phone rang again. It was Jake Watson, my editor.

"Ambrose tells me you have great plans for a special weekend feature."

"Yeah, right."

"It says right here in my turnover note, and I quote: 'Kate wants to talk to you about plans for the weekend feature.'"

"Let's rephrase that, boss. Kate knows she can't avoid

27

talking to you about plans for a weekend feature, especially as the publisher thinks the opposition is beating our ass."

"Well, that, too." Jake was laughing.

"What is there left to say? I've profiled everyone on the team, including the bat boys."

"There's got to be a new angle. Did anything come out of the trip?"

"Steve Thorson and his agent have split and the agent's pissed off. But there's not a whole story in that. There's some other minor stuff, too. I can give you a good notebook for Sunday if you like."

"Make it long. What else?"

"I guess I can't avoid the dreaded playoff pressure story. I could talk to some of the veterans about how to handle it. Guys who have been to the playoffs with other teams. I could frame it as advice to the younger players. It's not very original, but I'll try to do it as well as I can."

"That will work. Early next week?"

"You're okay for Sunday's paper?"

"I've got enough. But next week's going to be hairy, especially if they win this thing quick. Then people won't care about the game stories. We'll have to come up with something else."

"I'll do my best, boss, sir."

"Shut up, Kate. Will you be by the office before you go to the ballpark?"

"I doubt it, but you know where to find me. And, Jake?"

"Yeah?"

"I guess this means I won't be able to take any days off this weekend, eh?"

"I know, and isn't it a shame?"

I hung up smiling and went back to my mundane

chores. The feature on the veterans meant that I had to get to the ballpark early to do some interviews.

I took my second cup of tea up to my study, picking up my briefcase on the way. It was a fine leather bag that had been a present from Mickey. He thought it would help my image, but within a month it had looked as grotty as the old canvas carryall it had replaced. I guess God didn't mean for me to be tidy.

My study was a mess. Stacks of magazines and newspapers covered the floor and my desk was hidden under more debris, which I carefully transferred to the couch. I had once returned from a road trip and not realized my place had been ransacked in my absence until I'd been home for three hours.

Even with the mess, it was a beautiful room. I'd designed the renovations myself, turning an attic space into a large, bright studio with big windows and a skylight. One wall held bookcases, packed with mysteries and baseball books. Part of the opposite wall was mirrored and mounted with a short ballet barre. I had studied ballet seriously when I was younger, but puberty wiped out my ambitions. There isn't much call for ballerinas who are five foot nine and have boobs. Besides, I wasn't good enough. But I love to dance and still keep my hand, or toe, in as a way to keep a little bit fit. I loathe any other kind of exercise.

My desk, next to the window, is an old oak harvest table that spent its early life in a convent. I emptied my briefcase and kicked Elwy off my chair. While I sorted my notes, he lay on his back in the middle of the floor, meowing pathetically, demanding attention.

"Piss off, Elwy."

I was halfway down the basement stairs with my arms full of laundry when the phone rang again. Swearing,

I stumbled back up the steps, leaving a trail of undies Hansel and Gretel could have followed. When I answered the phone, I was glad I'd hurried. It was Christopher Morris, my favourite magazine writer, calling from New York.

"I'm coming to Toronto tomorrow. Can we get together for dinner? I need to pick your brain."

"The pennant race is now official, I guess. And you've been ignoring my fine boys all these years. Why should I help you?"

"Because you are a kind and generous human being. And because I'm buying dinner."

"There's a good reason. When do you get in?"

"In time for the game. I'll see you in the press box."

"I can't wait."

I couldn't. Christopher was one of the few sports-writers I admired without reservation. And, to tell the truth, I was flattered that he had called me.

It quite made my day.

4

I left for the ballpark at four, stopping at the corner store for cigarettes and to catch up on the gossip.

My neighbourhood is undergoing gentrification, becoming impossibly trendy. I liked it the way it was, a nice mix of working-class WASPs who had lived in their houses for generations and immigrants, mainly Greek, who add some colour. When the wind is blowing down from the restaurants on Danforth Avenue, the street smells like one big shiskebob, and I buy my meat at a butcher's with a whole sheep hanging in the window.

Now we're being invaded by yuppies and gays tearing the front porches off the old brick houses and putting up brass numbers under coach lights by their doors. Filipino and Swedish nannies walk blonde toddlers and designer dogs with kerchiefs around their necks. Real estate agents put enough crap through my door to insulate the attic with waste paper. There are more dumpsters on the street than fire hydrants, collecting the renovators' debris. The health-food store on the corner has expanded into a mall.

But they haven't taken away the view at the end of my street. Beyond the park and the Don Valley Parkway, the downtown skyline looked like the emerald city of Oz in the late afternoon sun. I crossed the Valley, once the easternmost boundary of civilized Toronto, past the Don Jail. As usual, there were film crew trucks parked outside the old stone wing, now used only as a stand-in for jails supposedly in New York or Boston.

I avoided downtown by going down Parliament Street to the Gardiner Expressway, then west along the bottom of the city, past the gleaming bank towers and the CN Tower, the postcard view of Toronto.

The stadium on the lakefront was all shut up in the middle of its empty parking lot, just one gate open for players and press. Inside, a huge corridor runs around the perimeter of the stadium, under the stands. It's big enough for trucks to drive in, always cool and a little spooky. My high heels echoed as I walked past the Titan clubhouse and down the umpires' tunnel to the field.

I remembered the first time I took this walk, how nervous and excited I was and how strange it seemed. Now it's as comfortable as my living room. And no wonder. I spend almost as much time there as I do at home.

There weren't many players out yet. Slick Marshall and Dummy Doran, two of the coaches, were sitting in their usual spots on the bench gazing grumpily at the field. They nodded as I dropped my gear and joined them.

"Afternoon, gentlemen. Lovely day."

Doran grunted.

"Any injuries I should know about?"

"I won't bother you with the details of my hangover," Marshall said. "I'll play with the pain."

32

He stood up and moved heavily towards the clubhouse. Doran followed him.

"Work to do," he lied.

As usual, they made me feel as welcome as the plague. Players started to straggle out of the clubhouse, styrofoam cups of coffee in hand. Some were more friendly.

Sultan Sanchez, the designated hitter, sat next to me and patted my knee.

"You lookin' good, baby. What about you and me after the game?"

"Sorry, Sultan. I've got to wash my hair."

This supposed seduction is a running gag I'm getting a bit tired of, but it's easier to keep it going than to try to explain why it offends me. Sultan wouldn't understand. In truth, I don't think he understands why I keep saying no.

Sultan's a complicated man. He's very handsome and very proud. He was born in the Dominican Republic either 42 or 46 years ago, depending on whom you believe, and is an enormous star at home. But he's never been as rich and famous as he thinks he deserves in the majors. Sanchez sees it all as a racist, anti-Latin conspiracy, and it has made him bitter; but his only real problems have been timing and talent. When he started to play no one made big salaries. And all he can do is hit. Various teams have tried to put him in the field, disastrously. He is a born designated hitter.

He is also lazy. Orca Elliott, the other designated hitter, at least goes through the pretence of taking infield practice every day. Sultan doesn't bother. He holds court in the dugout or clubhouse, depending on the weather, and tries to get extra swings in the batting cage.

During a game, he swaggers to the plate, where he either strikes out or hits a home run, the former more often than the latter these days. He also hits into double plays and never runs out a ground ball.

This is probably his last season. Ted Ferguson, the owner of the team, sees him as a bad influence on the younger Latin players. He's probably right. But still, there's a certain charm to the man, and he's still entertaining to watch. The fans love him.

"Sultan, you've been through this kind of thing before. What advice do you have for the players who have never been in the playoffs or World Series? Is it really that different?"

"Not for the Sultan," he boomed. "I don' know the meaning of the word pressure . . ."

And me without my English-Spanish dictionary.

"When I was with the Reds in the World Series I hit two home runs in one game. I should have been MVP . . ."

And if you hadn't been Latin you would have been.

"But you know they're not going to give no pretty car to Señor Sanchez from Santo Domingo."

I carry on these silent dialogues quite often. I can't say them out loud if I want the players to go on talking to me, but it helps me hold on to whatever sanity I have left.

I waited until he wound down the tales of past glory.

"What about the kids? Alex Jones is a rookie. Archie Griffin. How are they going to handle all the crowds and media attention?"

"Alejandro has been in the Caribbean World Series twice. You don' think we get big crowds down there? Man, those fans down there in the Dominican are crazy. They're more crazy in Santo Domingo than even they are in New Jork. Alejandro can handle it. Don' worry about a thing with Alejandro."

Other players had come onto the field as we were talking. Pitchers ran laps in the outfield; other players did stretching exercises, and a few began to play catch. The workday had begun, and Sanchez was getting antsy answering questions. He had to make his rounds and kibitz with everyone.

It was a getting-up sort of time at the ballpark, unguarded and private. The players cherished it. They were secure in a corner of the world they understood. Whether it was a sandlot in rural Arkansas, a rocky diamond retrieved from the rubble of a New York ghetto, or the finest major-league park, it was their sanctuary. And no time was more precious than the hours before the game when the whole joint belonged to them.

Later, the stands would fill with strangers, some friendly, others hostile, all filled with passionate and noisy expectations. Now it was peaceful, and no one demanded anything of anyone except indulgence in rituals as old as the game itself.

The few outsiders, the reporters and grounds-keepers, are tolerated because, in our own way, we're family. Annoying in-laws, perhaps, but family none-theless.

It's my favourite time at the ballpark, too. Even horrible Titan Field has its charms. It's a jerry-rigged affair, tacked on to the end of an existing football stadium when Toronto got its franchise. It has artificial turf, which I loathe, and half the seats in the place are bad. But I've seen a lot of games here and I'll miss it when it's torn down and replaced by something up to date.

A ball bounced off my foot.

"Heads up, Hank!"

"Okay, I'm awake!" I walked over and picked up the ball. Moose Greer waved a glove at me, motioning for the throw. He was playing catch with Toby King, an obnoxious little chirper who covered sports for a local television station. King was a Personality, from his blow-dried hair to the soles of his Adidas. In between, he was wearing a shirt with the logo of the Argonaut football team, a sweater supplied by a local tennis tournament, and a jacket compliments of Super Bowl XVII. I wondered where he got his underwear, but not enough to do any intimate research.

"Yo, King! Who said you could use my glove?"

"Sorry, Sultan. Do you have plans for it in the next ten minutes? Maybe you're going to take some ground balls? I'd pay to see that."

"You just take good care of it, midget."

King saluted him, laughing. I walked over to meet Steve Thorson, who was just coming off the field.

"Got a minute?"

"What do you want?"

"I'm doing a piece on post-season pressure."

"Sure. Let's do it inside."

I feared I was going to get the wise-veteran song and dance when all I wanted was a couple of quotes. But at least I'd caught him in a good mood. Some days he won't talk at all.

I followed him into the clubhouse, which is nothing like the image most people have of a locker room. There aren't even any lockers. Each player has a wooden cubicle about three feet wide, with hooks for his clothes and shelves for his hair drier, jock itch powder, cologne, and other necessities of the sporting life.

You can tell a lot about a player by his locker. Some are neat and bare. Others are crammed with junk. Some guys decorate their lockers with everything from lewd pin-ups to plaster statues of saints. Thorson is halfway in between. He had some extraneous stuff – a fishing rod, a football, a few boxes of fan mail. He'd also replaced his name in the slot on top of the cubicle with a hand-lettered sign reading "The Boss."

He sat in a director's chair with his name on the

back, a present from his wife, while I pulled up a stool from the next one over. I didn't even have to ask the questions.

"The playoffs and World Series are times that test the true strength of a man. Some rise to the pressure. Others get crushed by it. For me, it's when I feel the most alive."

Anyone who hasn't been there can't know it, I bet.

"If you've never been there before, you won't know what can happen. That's why it's an adventure. Every player wonders, will I excel or will I fail? Will I be the hero or the goat? Will my winter be long and cold or a time to remember happy things?"

Will I get a mess of new endorsements and bonuses?

I shouldn't be cynical. He was giving me good stuff. We talked, he talked, for twenty minutes. Just before we wrapped up I remembered the notebook I'd promised Jake for Sunday.

"One more thing. What's the situation with Sam Craven?"

His face closed right up.

"There is no situation. We're through."

"Your contract with him isn't up, is it?"

"He's fired. I've got someone else. End of comment."

"Who's your new agent?"

"End of comment. Period. That's it. None of your business. The interview is over."

I opened my mouth to speak.

"Go away," he said. I went.

I ran into Archie – Mark – Griffin in the hall with Flakey Patterson.

"Kate, this is great. You've got to see this."

Griffin handed me a piece of paper. It looked like a press release, except it was hand-printed. At the top of the page was a rubber-stamped impression of the logo

Flakey had designed for himself: a flamingo standing on its right leg, clutching a baseball in its left claw. The heading was in red.

"FOR IMMEDIATE RELEASE: PATTERSON VOWS TO WIN."

"What now, Flakey?"

He smiled enigmatically and made the child's sign of silence, locking his lips and throwing away an imaginary key. I went back to his release.

"Phil Patterson, the lefthanded genius of the Toronto Titans pitching staff, has taken dramatic action to ensure the team's clinching of the American League Eastern Division Championship.

"He has vowed to keep silent and maintain a partial fast until the crown is won. He will consume nothing but Gatorade, which he needs to balance electrolytes in his body.

"In a statement released yesterday, Patterson said, 'There is a sinister plot to keep the Titans from our destiny, and it is time for the lefthanders to take charge. Behind my inspirational leadership, the Toronto Titans will not be left behind. We will be left on top.'

"In addition to his usual arsenal of magic pitches and mind-boggling mantras, Patterson has received a powerful talisman from a faithful fan.

" 'Although I am opposed to maiming of animals for human folly, I am proud to carry this amulet,' he said. 'It is the left hind foot of a rare and holy Himalayan hare, dead of natural causes after a long life as the companion of a Buddhist monk. I will go nowhere without it.'

"After the Titans clinch their division, Patterson will break his fast with imported champagne."

"Nice, Flakey, really nice," I said, folding the paper and slipping it into my pocket. "I'll use this in my notebook."

He made a steeple of his fingers and bowed.

The press floor was a circus. Every two-bit newspaper and radio station in Ontario had someone covering the last week of the season. Winners attract attention, and the Titans had become the home team for an entire province, even the country. Major papers from Halifax to Vancouver were phoning in requests for credentials. The big-shot baseball writers from the States were starting to arrive. It was the only pennant race left in the league. The Oakland A's had won the Western Division Championship the previous week.

I wolfed down some lasagna and salad with a couple of reporters from Ottawa and a runner for the NBC television crew, then escaped to the relative peace of the press box. There was permanent space assigned to each of the regulars in the front row. Mine was right behind home plate, with Moose Greer to my left and Bill Sanderson from the *World* on my right.

The stadium was buzzing well before game time. The corporate boxes just below me were full of high rollers eating cold cuts and drinking Scotch. In the stands the common folk were eating bad hot dogs, drinking flat beer and having at least as much fun.

The festive mood lasted until the second pitch of the game, a home run for the Red Sox leadoff hitter. There were enough Boston fans in the park to raise a little ruckus, a joyful and gloating noise. The Red Sox were out of the race, but it didn't stop them from wanting to be spoilers.

Things never got better that chilly night. The Red Sox had a 4–0 lead by the time the Titans came to bat (and went down in order). Doc Dudley, the Titan starter, was gone by the third. The usually reliable fielders made three errors. To make things worse, the out-of-town scoreboard showed that the Yankees were beating the Indians. I began writing my story for the first edition, keeping one eye on the game. Watching them blow it made me bad-tempered.

So did writing the first-edition story. On Friday's early deadline it had to be in as soon as the game was over, so there was no chance for analysis, no telling what plays will be key. So I stuck to descriptions of how each team had scored their runs. Some hacks write that kind of stuff for a living, but it's nothing but space filler for me, to be replaced later by something with more colour and bite.

When the last out was made – Sultan Sanchez's third strikeout of the game with men on base – I sent the story to the home computer over the phone and checked to make sure it had arrived intact. I promised the night editor my next story, with quotes, by midnight.

That only gave me an hour, but when I got to the clubhouse it was locked. Angry reporters were arguing with the security guard, an amiable retiree who took the abuse stolidly.

"What's going on?"

"It seems that Mr. O'Brien is giving one of his fatherly pep talks," said Toby King. "The team is evidently in need of inspiration, so we're shut out."

"Shit."

The door to the dressing room wasn't very effectively soundproofed, and sound of the angry voices could be heard. In a few minutes, a clubhouse kid opened it and we filed in, adjusting our faces to a properly funereal expression. A losing dressing room is a minefield of recriminations and emotion, especially late in the season with so much on the line. It wouldn't do to smile. Someone might think you weren't taking the game seriously.

I went into O'Brien's office with the herd of reporters and waited for someone else to ask the first question. Red hadn't got his nickname from the colour of his hair, what there was left of it. He had what players call "the red ass," a fierce temper. One of the out-of-town writers broke the silence.

"What went wrong, Red?"

"What the fuck do you think went wrong? The pitchers couldn't pitch and the fielders couldn't field. So goddamn glad to be home they just blew it. Probably left it at home in bed with their fucking wives. If these guys want to win this thing, they'd better start paying fucking attention. They're paid enough to keep themselves in the game."

"The Yankees won tonight."

"I am aware that the fucking Yankees fucking won. I'm not fucking blind."

A radio reporter moved around the desk to stick a microphone in front of him.

"Get that fucking thing out of my face. So we lost tonight. Big fucking deal. Even if the goddamn Yankees don't lose another game, all we have to win is four more.

That's so hard? That's impossible? Don't break your ankles jumping off the bandwagon, you fucking assholes."

He punctuated his last statement by firing a beer into the wastebasket. It shattered. There were no further questions. We were barely out of the office when he slammed the door and more crashes and bangs came from behind it. I stuck my head in the equipment manager's office.

"I hope you're ready for a long night. The boss is trashing his office again."

"And me with a hot lady waiting at home."

"Hey, what's more important? Sex or the pennant race?"

I went into the clubhouse, looking for Alex Jones. He'd won a spot on *This Week in Baseball*, but not for the reason he would have liked. In the fifth inning, with one out and men on first and second, he had fielded a routine ground ball and stepped on second base for what should have been the first half of a double play. But instead of relaying the ball to Tiny Washington, he tossed it over his shoulder to the second-base umpire, thinking that the inning was over, and started to run off the field. The umpire, of course, let the ball roll into centre field and the alert runner scampered home.

I found him at his locker, where he was denying any knowledge of the English language. He then put his towel around his neck and walked to the shower, winking at me as he passed.

The dressing room was half empty. Dudley wasn't there, nor was Sanchez. The game's biggest culprits were waiting us out in the trainer's room, which was off-limits to the press.

I had neither the time nor the inclination to hang around, so I collected some quotes from Gloves Gardiner about the game Dudley had pitched. Gloves never ducks the press.

I wrote and filed my story at the ballpark and was home by one, but was nowhere near ready for bed. One of the drawbacks of the job is the time it takes to wind down after writing, at an hour when most people are asleep. I was checking out late movies when there was a knock on the door.

It was Sally Parkes with a bottle of wine in hand.

"Hi, kiddo. Welcome home. I waited up."

"Bless your heart, Sal."

"What happened out there tonight? We watched the game."

"Who knows. How's T.C.?"

"Inconsolable. And on top of the loss, his wretched father cancelled out again this weekend. They were supposed to go to both games."

"I can get tickets for him. What happened to Roger?"

"He says he had to go to a strategy conference in Windsor, but I suspect it has something to do with the researcher from the Auto Workers he's currently screwing."

"Don't worry. I'll call in the morning. Two seats?"

"That would be great. I really appreciate it, Kate."

"I'll steer some players in his direction for an autograph if you get there early."

I like doing things for T.C. He's a nice, shy kid who hasn't had a lot of breaks. He's small for his age, wears glasses, and is a target for all the bullies. If he can get some prestige because he knows some ballplayers I'm delighted.

Sally opened the wine while I changed out of my work uniform and into sweats. We put the wine on the coffee table and, as we had so many nights before, curled up on opposite sofas and settled in for a gab.

I missed the company of women on the road.

"Okay, tell all," she said, grinning wickedly. "How was Mr. Same Time Next Year?"

"Same as last year."

I'd been having an odd affair with a Detroit columnist for five years. Sally couldn't understand why we confined our activities to my semi-annual trips with the team, but it suited us just fine.

"And I saw Tim in New York for lunch. But other than a couple of pub crawls in Chicago with the other writers it was pretty uneventful. A lot of hanging around the hotel bar listening to coaches tell the same old stories."

"How did the players treat you?"

"Same as usual. Stinger was more obnoxious than usual and David Sloane made a big scene in the clubhouse in New York again."

"You'd think he would have figured out by now that you're not in there to ogle."

"If I was, I wouldn't be ogling him, that's for sure."

Sloane, the centre fielder, is a Mormon who thinks that a woman in the clubhouse is an abomination against God and that I am Satan incarnate. It gets a bit boring. For years I've been trying to sneak the same typo into print: "David Sloane is a devout Moron." No luck so far.

"He's been fine for months. I guess it's the much vaunted pennant race pressure."

"Is that for real?"

"I don't know. Some of the players have been acting strangely lately. There are more short tempers in the clubhouse. There was almost a fight on the plane coming home between Steve Thorson and Joe Kelsey because he made an error. It's not much fun these days."

"These guys are bigger prima donnas than artists."

"Right about now I'd trade jobs with you in a second."

"No thanks. Except for all those naked men you get to ogle."

I threw my pillow at her.

I was leaning against the batting cage at noon the next day, talking with a Boston writer, when Tiny Washington ambled by.

"There's a gentleman admirer here for you," he said.

I turned to look where he was pointing, and saw T.C. in the stands next to the dugout waving at me, Titan cap on his head, a baseball glove on his left hand, and a pen clutched in his right. I waved and went to join him.

"Hi, Kate," he said. "My Mum said I could come down and say hi as long as I didn't bother you."

"You never bother me, kid." I refrained from kissing him. He had recently decided that kissing wasn't cool. "Long time no see. I missed you."

Tiny joined us and stuck out his huge hand to the boy.

"How's my little man," he said.

"Fine, Mr. Washington."

"Mr. Washington! You hear that, Kate? Here's someone who knows how to respect his elders. You can call me Tiny, son."

T.C. blushed.

"Are you going to win today?"

"Don't you worry. Tell you what I'm going to do. If I hit a home run, you get the bat."

"Gee, thanks, Mr. Washington. Tiny."

"What lies are you telling now?" Sultan Sanchez joined the group. "Don't listen to anything that man says. I'm the home-run hitter today. Sid Fiore's too tough for Tiny."

"Hi, Mr. Sanchez. Will you sign my glove?"

"Let me see that. This little thing? You're growing up too big for a kid's glove. Wait right here."

He ducked into the dugout and came back with his own glove.

"You've got more use for this than I do," he said.

"Oh, boy! Thanks, Mr. Sanchez!"

"You're welcome. Where are you sitting? I want to be able to see you after I get my home run."

T.C. pointed out where Sally was sitting, halfway up the section behind the Titan dugout. She waved. Sultan doffed his cap and bowed deeply, never missing a chance to flirt.

"Go show her your glove, sweetie," I said. "We've all got work to do."

His feet hardly touched the steps.

"That was nice, Sultan. You've made his day."

"Any time you want to pay back the favour, you know where to find me," he said, winking.

I found Tony Costello slumped in a corner of the dugout.

"I feel lousy, Kate. I don't know if I'll be able to pitch. I think I ate some bad food."

"You always feel lousy before you start. You'd feel

sick if your mom packed your lunch wearing sterilized gloves. You'll be fine after the first pitch."

How many times had I told him that? Sometimes I feel like a den mother.

"This is a big game. We've gotta win today."

"You don't gotta anything, Tony. What's going to happen if you lose? Is someone going to drop dead? Will the sun refuse to rise tomorrow morning? Hey, it's only a game."

Costello looked at the field, where a Red Sox hitter was knocking batting practice balls out of the park, and groaned.

He must have been feeling better by game time. He struck out the side in the top of the first. Then the fun began. Carter led off for the Titans with a single. Once at first, he inched towards second, bent at the knees and waist, grinning at Sid Fiore, the Red Sox pitcher.

Fiore was one of the best lefthanders in the league. Slim and handsome, he surprised with the power of his pitches, fastballs and sliders that were baffling when he was on his game. He was enough of a veteran not to let himself get rattled by Carter's antics, but threw to first a couple of times before setting his attention on Billy Wise, waiting at the plate.

On the first pitch, a pitchout, Carter was off. The throw to second was in time, but on the wrong side of the bag. The second-base umpire, Max Leonard, signalled safe.

Carter signalled for time out and got to his feet, calmly brushing the dirt off the front of his uniform, then strolled back towards first to retrieve his batting helmet.

Marty Hogan, the Red Sox manager, came out of the visitors' dugout, hands in his jacket pockets. Carter stood on second, his face impassive, his eyes flashing with excitement.

Fiore gestured to his catcher and began a soft game of catch, keeping his arm loose. Wise leaned on his bat and chatted with the home-plate umpire. The centre fielder hunkered down on his haunches.

In the meantime, Leonard was making himself dizzy. After listening to Hogan's argument for what he considered long enough, he turned his back on the enraged manager, but Hogan ran around to face him. Leonard kept turning, avoiding the argument. He didn't want to toss the manager in such a crucial game, despite advice from the Titans fans. Finally, he marched into centre field while his colleague from first cut Hogan off like a sheep-herding dog and sent him back to the dugout. The fans gave Hogan a derisive ovation.

The delay bothered Fiore. He walked Wise on three more pitches, picked up the resin bag, and threw it to the ground. He walked behind the mound and turned his back to the plate. He tucked his glove underneath his left arm and massaged the ball between his hands, gazing at the centre-field scoreboard. He took a deep breath, turned, and strode to the mound to face Joe Kelsey, always a home-run threat. Fiore pitched him carefully, working the count to two balls and two strikes. Kelsey fouled off pitch after pitch, waiting for the one he liked, then tapped a ground ball past the third baseman for a single. Carter held up at third, the bases were loaded, and the fans were on their feet.

Sultan Sanchez was up next. He stood at the plate and glared at Fiore, who nicked the outside corner for strike one, then wasted one high and inside. The crowd was chanting: "SUL-TAN, SUL-TAN." The Red Sox fielders were shifted towards left. He was a dead pull hitter — never hit a ball to the right side of field — and most teams played him that way. The Red Sox shift was so extreme their second baseman and shortstop were both stationed between second and third.

He fouled the third pitch off, then stepped out of the batter's box for a moment and glanced into the stands, towards where T.C. and Sally were sitting. Once back in the box, he dug in his cleats and waved his bat menacingly over his head, waiting for the pitch.

It came, he swung mightily and missed, going down on one knee with the effort. The crowd groaned as Sanchez trudged back to the dugout, twirling his bat in frustration, then threw his helmet against the bat rack.

Pumped up, Fiore watched Washington step to the plate. A lefthanded hitter, he was less of a problem. He had hit only four of his season's twenty-seven home runs off lefthanders, and had never hit well against Fiore.

Maybe Fiore relaxed just a bit too much. Washington pounded his first pitch over the right-field fence. Showing no emotion, he trotted slowly around the base-paths to home plate, where Carter, Wise, and Kelsey waited to welcome him. As it turned out, the game was won.

Between innings, I went to the dining room for a cup of tea. I stopped at the press box door on the way back.

My home away from home it might be, but it's an awful place to spend time. The architects, worried about our well-being early and late in the season, sealed us in behind plate glass. It's a hothouse from June until August, but even when it's chilly outside, the glass is only a mixed blessing.

It keeps out the cold, certainly. But it also keeps out the sounds of the game and keeps in the rather unique pollution of jock journalists. I can't in all conscience complain about the cigarette smoke, as some of it is my own, but the cheap cigars are foul. Their fumes are enriched by a subtle hint of undeodorized armpit and uncontrolled flatulence.

I found Christopher Morris in the back row and sat next to him for a few innings. We agreed to meet for dinner at eight.

Costello pitched shutout ball until the ninth. He loaded the bases then, on a pair of singles and a walk, and Griffin came in to get the final out for the twenty-first save of his rookie season.

But the crowd saved its biggest ovation for the scoreboard flashing the message that the Indians had beaten the Yankees, 8–2, in Cleveland.

Afterwards, the Titan clubhouse was jumping. I went to Costello's locker, where he sat, a towel wrapped around his corpulent midriff. He had a cigarette in one hand and a beer in the other and greeted me jubilantly, hooking a stool from the next locker with his right foot.

"Sit down. I should have listened to you."

"No fair, Bony. Now I can't say 'I told you so.' "

"The worse I am before the game, the better I feel when I start to pitch." He took a long swallow of beer. "And the guys made it easy for me today. I could kiss Tiny Washington right now!"

He directed the last statement loudly towards the first baseman's locker. Tiny looked up and waved.

"Except I don't want to catch whatever he's got," continued Costello. "It sure turns you ugly."

Washington took a mock run towards Costello's locker, growling. Suddenly, skinny Alex Jones leaped between them, naked as a newborn.

"No, Tiny," he shouted, raising his little fists. "If you hit him you will have to answer to me!"

Washington stopped, then raised his arms protectively in front of his face and cowered back to his locker.

"No, no! Anything but that!"

I followed him.

"Yankees lost?"

"They sure did."

"Never thought I'd be rooting for the Indians. I want to get this thing over with. I don't want it to come down to the last series."

"Tiny, where's your sense of drama?"

"I'm too old for drama. You know that."

"You can clinch it tomorrow with a bit of luck. You win, the Indians win, and it's done."

"That would be sweet."

"How many grand slams have you hit?"

"Not enough. I don't like them, though," he deadpanned.

"Why not?"

"Too many handshakes. By the time I've figured out the high five, low five, soul shake, Latin shake, and plain old white bread handshake, I'm worn out."

Sultan Sanchez interrupted from the next locker.

"I softened him up for you, Tiny. I should get half that dinger."

"Now I know where you got them brown eyes, Sultan. You're full of shit."

I turned to leave them to it, but Tiny stopped me.

"Take this to the boy," he said, handing me his bat.

I had time to go home and relax for an hour before going out to dinner. I took the streetcar to my favourite restaurant, the Fillet of Soul, a dark, cosy, barn-like place specializing in ribs and fried chicken, southern-style cooking transplanted north. I liked it for more than the food. I could drop in any time and find friends.

I was talking to Sarah Jefferson when Christopher arrived. She and her husband Tom had owned the restaurant for twenty years. He came to Toronto from Alabama to play football, met Sarah his first season, and decided to spend his life with her. That he was black and she white and the time the early sixties had made her home town a more comfortable place than his. When he began to miss his grandmother's cooking, he opened the restaurant and shared the cuisine with the rest of the city. Ontario was an unlikely place for soul food, but the restaurant had thrived.

"Were you there this afternoon? What a game! I cheered so hard I can hardly talk. Tiny's here, with

Darlene." Sarah was dithering. "I put them in the back room. And some of the Red Sox are here, too."

"Slip some ptomaine into their okra, and do us all a favour," I said, then introduced Christopher.

Sarah greeted him warmly, showed us to a table in the corner, took our drink orders, and left us alone.

"She's a bit nuts," I explained. "We're not used to winning in Toronto. We've got a bad hockey team and a football team just good enough to break our hearts year after year."

"I don't know what anyone's worried about. You've got four good starters and great hitting. The Yankees are done. Jimmy Fox has burned out the bullpen in the last two weeks."

"Don't confuse me with logic. This is the biggest battle since the War of 1812. That's the last time we beat you guys."

"Well, we could use a bit of that," Morris chuckled. "God knows the Yankees could. I'm rooting for the Titans."

The waiter came with the menus. I reached absently for one, then did a double take. Tiny Washington, with a napkin draped over his arm, bowed.

"The martini is for you, I believe, Miss Henry. And the Scotch is for Mr. Morris. We are honoured that you have chosen to grace our city with your presence."

Morris got up to greet him.

"How are you, Tiny? I haven't seen you in years."

"No complaints. The old body's slowing down a bit, but I don't need speed for my home-run trot."

"You're being too modest, Tiny," I said. "Tell him about the bunt you beat out last week in Chicago."

"Yes, that's true," he laughed. "Only in the interests of honesty I have to point out that the third baseman was playing me halfway to second. The old Washington

54

Shift. But don't let me disturb you folks any more. I've got to get my rest."

"There's one wonderful guy," I said after he left. "I don't know how I would get along without him."

"The Titans are lucky to have him in the clubhouse," Morris agreed. "I remember him when he first came up with the Mets. He had that avuncular quality at nineteen."

Dinner was relaxed and pleasant. Morris was almost twenty years my senior, but he was neither world-weary nor stuffy. He was a small island of humanity in the sea of cynicism that is the press box.

Over sloppy ribs and collard greens, I filled him in on the colour he was looking for, about the team and the town.

"What's the story with Steve Thorson?" he asked, when the pecan pie arrived.

"Who knows? Maybe he's washed up."

"He's been a great pitcher for so long it's hard to believe he's mortal."

"I figure it looks good on him."

"You don't like him?"

"Do you?"

"He's always pretty quotable, and not stupid about the game. I've had some good conversations with him."

"Well, you don't see him every day. The endless analysis gets tedious. Besides, it all always comes down to how everybody else is to blame."

"I thought he was popular."

"The fans love him. He's always ready to front a charity or sign autographs, but it's all phoney. I've never seen a spontaneous gesture out of the man. He goes to visit Sick Kids' Hospital, you can be sure there's a television camera there."

"Do you know the problems he's having with his agent?"

"Sam Craven? Just that he's dumped him. What else?"

"That's enough. You don't dump Sam Craven, especially when you're negotiating a new contract. Sam wants his piece.

"His ego is also at stake. He prides himself on representing the best athletes in all sports. The people I talk to say that if Thorson gets away, the others are going to be watching very carefully. And if Thorson can get the contract he wants without Craven, a lot of them will walk."

"What can Craven do?" I asked.

"Do you remember a basketball player named Danny Marx? He signed with Craven when he was still in college."

"He was a first-round draft pick in the NBA about five years ago, wasn't he? Whatever happened to him?"

"He committed suicide in prison last year, after being convicted of possession of heroin. He swore his innocence right to the end. That much is public knowledge. What isn't known is that Marx was a clean-living, God-fearing kid who made the mistake of trying to wriggle out of his contract with Craven."

"What do you mean?"

"He wanted to put his money into a Christian Action investment plan. Craven tried to fight it, but Marx had the fervour of a born-again and wouldn't listen. He said Craven was an agent of Satan. The summer before he was arrested, Marx began dating a young woman he had met at church. They planned to marry that fall.

"She was at the trial every day, quite the devoted fiancée. When Danny went to jail, she dropped out of sight. Now she has surfaced as the owner of a small casino on one of the smaller Caribbean islands. She didn't buy it on her salary as a stenographer. And, needless to say, she had a key to his apartment, where the evidence to convict him was found."

"Craven?"

"Or one of his mob buddies. I hope Thorson knows what he's getting into."

The conversation was starting to give me the creeps. I live a fairly sheltered life. In my world, the really bad people park in spaces reserved for the handicapped. This stuff was straight out of Elmore Leonard. I wasn't ready for it to leap off the pages into the life of someone I knew. Still, I was fascinated.

"What's Craven like? I've never met him."

"He's charming," Morris said. "He doesn't wear black shirts and white ties. His aides don't carry violin cases. He's very smooth, very amusing, an excellent story-teller, and he just walked into the restaurant."

"He just what?"

"He's standing at the door with Bert Nelson from ABC." Morris smiled at my discomfort. "Do you want to meet him?"

"Oh, Jesus, I don't know. I guess so. Yes, why not?"

Morris stood up and waved, as I turned to look. I recognized Nelson. The man with him was tall, tanned, and handsome, dressed in an oxford-cloth shirt, jeans, and a good tweed sports jacket. He looked to be in his forties, with a few lines softening the angles of his face. When he spotted Morris, he smiled, with his mouth and his eyes, and crossed the restaurant with his hands outstretched.

"Chris, good to see you. In town for the big game?"

Morris performed the introductions, and the smile swung around to include me in its beam.

"Ah, the famous Ms Henry. I've been reading your stories for years. You write rings around most of the men."

I could feel the blush rising up my neck, an unfortunate affliction I'd never been able to conquer. Craven didn't seem to notice.

"Is this a private party, or can we join you?"

Not waiting for a reply, he motioned to Nelson and pulled out the chair next to me and ordered cognacs all around.

"I'll turn it around, Sam," Morris said. "What are you doing here? Toronto's not your usual weekend haunt."

"I've come to watch my favourite client pitch tomorrow. I have to keep track of my investments."

I bit my tongue.

"I think the Titans are going all the way. Thorson's going to prove what a money pitcher he is in the next few weeks. Bert and his network might not like a Canadian team in the World Series, but I think it's good to shake things up."

I couldn't ignore a second opening.

"I'm surprised at your interest," I said. "I thought Steve Thorson was no longer a client."

"That's just a game, Kate. Steve and I are engaged in a bit of ceremonial sabre-rattling."

Christopher was right. I spent a lovely hour listening to the three of them tell stories, each one funnier than the last. When Craven called for another round, I looked at my watch.

"Not for me, unless you want to watch me nap with my head on the table," I said. "I have to be back at the ballpark in less time than I care to think about. Thanks anyway."

"We'll do it another time, then." He stood up and extended his hand. "Maybe dinner during the playoffs."

"If the Titans make the playoffs, I'm afraid it's going to be sandwiches on the run for me."

"That is almost enough to make me root for the Yankees," he said, finally letting go of my hand. I simpered like an idiot.

"Christopher, I'll let you find your own way back to the hotel, if you don't mind." I leaned over and kissed him on the cheek. "I'll see you all at the ballpark tomorrow."

I stopped in the bar to say good night to Tom and Sarah. They were sitting at their usual corner table with a blonde I'd seen before.

"Say hi to Ginny," Tom said. "It's her birthday."

At least her forty-fifth was my guess, although her leather miniskirt and low-cut silk blouse denied it. Her hair was freshly tinted and tousled and she wore enough gold to dazzle a blind man, but nothing could disguise the softness of her jaw line and wrinkles around her eyes.

Sarah walked me to the door.

"I could kill Sultan Sanchez," she said.

"Why, because he struck out?"

"No. Ginny. He stood her up tonight, the prick."

"She should know better. He's a sleaze."

"I know, but still . . . By the way, who is that man?"

"I introduced you. Christopher Morris."

"No, not him. The gorgeous one who was drooling all over you when you were leaving."

"His name is Sam Craven, he's Steve Thorson's agent, and he wasn't drooling."

"Kate, trust my eyes if you don't trust yours. The man is definitely interested in you."

"Don't be ridiculous," I said, as a cab pulled up. "He's not my type even if he is."

"Whatever you say, sweetie," she said, hugging me.

As the taxi bounced along the streetcar tracks heading home, I thought about Sam Craven. I had been expecting Edward G. Robinson and got Paul Newman instead. And Sarah had been right. He had certainly seemed interested.

If half of what Christopher had told me was true, he wasn't someone I wanted anywhere near me. But still, it was a bit of a kick. Maybe I would have dinner with him. If nothing else, I might get a story out of it.

3

Sunday morning was grey, with rain in the air, and by eleven it had started to drizzle. When I got to the ballpark, the players were in a chapel meeting in the clubhouse – a weekly exercise in hypocrisy for half of them and evangelical overkill for the rest. I waited in the dugout, smoking cigarettes and reading the paper. I wanted to see Thorson before the game.

When the meeting broke up and the pious and pseudo-pious came out, I went into the clubhouse to find him. He was sitting by his locker, but when he saw me coming he got up and headed towards the hall, brushing past me on the way.

Steeling myself, I followed him, catching up in the hall.

"Sorry to bother you, Steve," I said, ignoring his mood. "I'd like to talk for just a minute."

He whirled around and glared.

"Can't it wait until after I've pitched?"

"It will only take a few minutes."

He folded his arms and leaned against the wall.

"I thought you said you and Sam Craven were through."

"We are."

"Not according to him."

"What are you talking about?"

"He's in town. I met him last night."

"He's here?"

"He said you'd have everything straightened out by the end of the week."

"That bastard."

"He said he was coming to watch you pitch today."

"I can't talk about this horseshit. I've got to get ready to pitch."

He went back into the dressing room as Moose Greer came out.

"What was that all about?"

"I think it might have something to do with my telling him that Sam Craven is in town."

"Yeah. He called me for a ticket," he said. "Listen, have you seen Sultan?"

"Not today. Hasn't he showed up?"

"You know Sultan. There's a righthander pitching. He's not scheduled to play."

"Still, that's cutting it a bit fine, even for him. Maybe he's sick. He stood up a date at the Fillet last night."

"He probably had a better offer. He'll show up."

I went back into the dressing room. It was full of players who would have been taking batting practice except for the rain. Instead, they were hanging around inside, full of nervous energy, playing cards or horsing around. There was an edge to all the activity, a tension. Voices were just a bit loud, the banter a bit forced. It was exciting.

I went to talk to Tiny.

"All ready for the big game?"

"I've been here before. Worry about the youngsters."

"I just wish it was game time right now," said Joe Kelsey, from the next locker. "I can't stand the wait. I was up at six o'clock this morning."

"You're lucky," said Eddie Carter. "I didn't sleep at all. The baby was sick."

Kelsey got up from the stool and wandered in his shower sandals to a table in the middle of the room, where he sat down and began signing baseballs.

"I feel like throwing up and I'm not even starting today," said Doc Dudley. Flakey Patterson nodded his silent agreement vehemently.

"Flakey, you're nuts. You haven't got anything in your stomach to throw," laughed Mark Griffin. "If we don't win today, you're going to get pretty hungry."

He turned around and addressed the clubhouse at large, making grand gestures.

"All right, guys, listen up," he said.

"Listen to yourself, rook," shouted Stinger Swain.

"We can't drag this thing out any longer," Griffin said, ignoring him. "We've got to win it for our own Gipper, Mr. Phil Patterson Esquire. The man is starving."

"Veronica could stand to lose a few pounds," shouted Swain. "It might improve his pitching!"

Patterson looked mournfully at his tormentor.

"Might even make him normal!" chimed in David Sloane.

"Forget it," laughed Gloves Gardiner. "That would be like the Pope getting married."

"Or Thorson getting humble," said Swain.

Thorson's sense of humour wasn't his strong point, especially when he was the butt of the joke. He glared at Swain and left the room, pausing to speak softly to Joe Kelsey, who jumped to his feet, fists clenched. Eddie Carter jumped between them and led Kelsey away. Thorson went into the trainer's room.

"What the hell is going on?" asked Tiny Washington in the sudden silence.

"Nothing, Tiny," Kelsey said, shaking his head. "I'm a bit jumpy today. Let's just get the darn thing over with."

"What did he say?" I joined the group.

"Drop it, Kate. I don't want this all over the papers."

"Okay, so I won't print it. Tell me what he said."

"Just a crack about my glove. Forget it. I shouldn't let him get to me."

He walked away. Tiny and I went up the runway to the dugout. He looked out at the soggy field, gnawing on his thumbnail, a sure sign of his tension.

"I don't like the way things feel this morning," he said. "Everybody's too tense. Damn Thorson."

"He just won't let up on Preacher," I said. "But it's not just Preacher. Everybody's nervous when he's pitching, these days. They're so afraid to make mistakes they can't relax and do their jobs. But what's the big deal? You guys are professionals. You're paid money to win games. One person can't change that. Besides, he's the best pitcher you've got."

"You're right. How come you're so smart?"

He grinned and went back inside.

Red O'Brien was in the dugout, sitting by the water cooler with one foot up on the bench. He had a whole new audience of reporters and was loving the attention. Those of us who covered the team regularly had long ago stopped listening to him.

O'Brien wasn't much of a manager. He had been one of the original Titans chosen in the expansion draft, an aging third baseman the Yankees could find no compelling reason to protect. But he was a favourite of Ted Ferguson's so he had played a couple of seasons. When his playing career ended, he was sent to the Titan minor-league system to manage his way back to the big leagues. This was his first season as major-league manager, and there were those who jumped to the conclusion that his leadership had something to do with the team's success. They were wrong.

But the reporters from Owen Sound and Thunder Bay didn't know that. Nor, for that matter, did the ones from the American national magazines. O'Brien was young, he was colourful, and he'd been a Yankee.

"What about pressure, Red? Can your team handle it?"

The reporter looked to be about twenty, and nervous. Feeling the pressure, no doubt. O'Brien shifted his tobacco chaw in his right cheek, leaned sideways, and spat.

"An old manager of mine gave me one bit of advice when I took this job. He told me to play one game at a time. Well, that seemed like pretty good advice then, and it still does. We got lots of time to win two games. One, if the Yankees and Indians co-operate."

"It's a young team, though, Red. They've never been through it before. I've seen young teams fold under this kind of pressure."

"I'm proud as can be of all my boys. If they're looking for a most valuable player on this team, they're not going to be able to give away a car. It's gonna have to be a bus, because every man on this team deserves it. That's what we are, a team. Each man makes his contribution, even on the bench, and I know that every one of them is pulling for everyone else."

I wasn't sure whether I was going to get the giggles or throw up, so I started for the press box. Christopher Morris joined me.

"The ol' philosopher's in good form today."

"I think I've heard it all before."

"Who hasn't? Let's get some lunch."

Over lukewarm scrambled eggs and grey sausages, I told Christopher about my conversation with Thorson.

"Either Craven's a good bluffer or Thorson hasn't communicated with him very well. He seemed pretty calm about it last night."

"Well, I wouldn't play poker with the man. They going to get this game in today?"

"Probably. They can suck the water off this field in half an hour. One blessing of artificial turf, unless you happen to be a fan sitting in the rain. They never call games around here unless it's really pouring."

When we went into the press box, the Zamboni was indeed vacuuming the outfield while the ground crew took the tarpaulin off the infield. Players were playing catch in front of the dugouts, stretching, and running short sprints.

"The weather office says we're clear for three hours," said Moose Greer.

"Great. Just call down to the clubhouse and tell them to play fast."

The press box was filling up, as were the stands. The fans filing down the aisles were crazy with anticipation. Some of the younger ones had painted their faces blue and white and waved grotesque giant foam fingers in the air and yelled stuff about being number one. The older fans were more sedate, some positively grim. They weren't going to celebrate prematurely. The anthems were sung by a local barbershop quartet. It was rumoured that Ted Ferguson was having an affair with their publicist, so they sang the anthems a lot. We stood in the press box, continuing our conversations out of the sides of our mouths, anxious to get back to our keyboards. I was in my seat before the last "stand on guard" had finished reverberating.

"Got your game face on, Henry?" asked Jeff Glebe,

the lead columnist on the *Planet*, wedging his long legs under the counter that served as a desk.

"Hey, I came to watch," I said, "and I'm planning to give it 110 per cent. I just hope I can stay within myself."

The Titans ran on the field as the crowd roared. I focused my binoculars on each one in turn.

Tiny Washington was the first out of the dugout, waving to the crowd as he trotted to first base. Alex Jones was next, rookie nerves making his eyes huge. Then Stinger Swain, glowering fiercely. Billy Wise went to his place at shortstop calmly and stood grooming the dirt with his spikes.

The outfielders ran out together, then split three ways, like an aerobatics team in mid-display. Preacher Kelsey looked determined as he went to left field, phlegmatic David Sloane jogged to centre field as if he was out for a Sunday run in the park. Eddie Carter covered his nerves with a deceptive exuberance, detouring to chat with Washington, the first-base umpire, and Jones before getting to right field, where he exchanged quips with the fans in the stands.

After Gloves Gardiner strolled to his station behind home plate, the captain on the bridge of his ship, Steve Thorson came out of the runway and sprinted to the mound. The fans were on their feet cheering, and the players in the dugout joined the applause.

"Hardly exciting at all, eh, kid?"

Jeff is one of the few sportswriters I know who admits to enjoyment of the moment.

Thorson's first pitch was a strike, a slider that barely nicked the inside corner. I sensed relief all over the stadium. Thorson had it.

Unfortunately, Ron Haskell, the Red Sox leadoff hitter, had it, too. He lashed a single to right field and promptly stole second.

Thorson picked up the resin bag just so he could throw it down in disgust. He glared at Gloves, even though Haskell had stolen the base on his delivery. There wasn't a catcher in baseball who could have thrown Haskell out with the lead he had taken.

Thorson's next pitch almost went by Gardiner, and the crowd began to stir uneasily. The third pitch was high, and Gardiner ran to the mound. The two consulted briefly and angrily. Gloves does not like being shown up. With a three and one count, I half expected them to walk Teddy Amaro to set up a double play, but Thorson came back with a fastball across the heart of the plate, which Amaro watched, and followed it with a changeup Amaro flailed at for the third strike.

I didn't know the next player. Randy Slaughter was playing first in place of Dave Marsden, who had a bad knee. The media notes said he'd just been called up three days earlier. He was a nineteen-year-old who had never played higher than Double A ball. He hailed from Needle's Eye, Virginia.

"Now there's a thriving metropolis for you."

"I bet the whole town's watching the game," Jeff said. "All four of them."

"Hey, let's not knock small towns," Moose said. "I have a ballpark named after me in Vulture Gulch."

"Vulture Gulch? Where the hell is Vulture Gulch?"

"It's hard by Rooster Creek, down the pike from Bob's Corner."

"You Yanks come up with some great names, Moose."

"Vulture Gulch is funnier than South Porcupine? Well, excuuuse me."

In the meantime, Mr. Needle's Eye had singled to left field. Kelsey's throw held Haskell at third, but with one out, there were a lot of ways he could score. It got very quiet in the stadium.

Bobby Johnson was the designated hitter. He was

an arrogant jerk, a high-priced free agent who thought he was worth the money he was paid. Worse, he was a great hitter. I'd seen him win a lot of games.

The fans booed. Johnson dug in and gazed impassively at Thorson. It was a meeting of massive egos. I wasn't sure which of them I liked less. Under the circumstances, I had to root for Thorson.

"Why are they booing? They'll just get him mad."

Thorson's first pitch brushed Johnson back. He glared at the mound and defiantly dug in again. The second pitch was at his throat. Here was the intimidation implicit in the game, laid out naked and ugly for all the world to see.

When Thorson's third pitch was in exactly the same place, the fans grew quiet. Johnson stepped back into the box and swung his bat gently, finishing the motion by pointing it at Thorson's head.

Thorson took the sign from Gardiner impatiently.

"He's got to walk him," Glebe muttered. "He can't pitch to him now."

"There's no way he's going to back down."

The next pitch was a fastball right down the middle. Johnson swung so hard he fell to one knee, missing the ball entirely, and the bat flew out of his hand, towards the mound. Thorson waited for Johnson to walk to the mound to retrieve it, then picked it up and poked him in the chest with it.

This was getting exciting.

The next pitch was a slider that nicked the outside corner for a called strike. Max Leonard gave the call a little bit extra as Johnson glowered at him in disbelief.

Some fans were on their feet clapping rhythmically as Thorson set again.

"I don't believe this," Glebe said.

Thorson then threw the hardest pitch I'd ever seen him throw. He completely overpowered Johnson, whose swing missed the ball by a foot. The umpire rung him up emphatically.

"Holy shit," said Jeff. I concurred.

Right fielder Barry Redmond came to the plate without much enthusiasm and popped up the first pitch. He slammed his bat down in disgust and walked off the field without watching Gardiner catch it to end the half inning.

The game never got easier. It was still scoreless by the bottom of the seventh. Eddie Carter led off. The Red Sox pitcher was Harry Grimes, a crafty old veteran who threw an assortment of junk that looked as if I could hit it, and he made the the Titans look like chumps. Carter is what's known in the game as an aggressive hitter – a player so impatient he swings at everything – and had twice grounded out on bad pitches.

He had obviously decided to wait the pitcher out this time. Grimes started him off with big lazy curveball that missed outside. Carter was twitching with the effort not to swing at it. The next pitch was a strike, followed by two balls. The fifth pitch was what Grimes laughingly referred to as his fastball, motoring right in there at about 75 miles an hour.

That was the first of seven pitches Carter fouled off, protecting the plate and waiting for his chance. It was a gutsy performance, and he was rewarded for it. The thirteenth pitch was in the dirt, and Grimes kicked angrily at the rubber as Carter sprinted to first.

Next up was Alex Jones, who was batting .312, but without much power. He was batting left against the righthanded Grimes and bounced the first pitch directly at the second baseman for a routine double play. A groan ran around the ballpark, with a scattering of boos.

David Sloane singled up the middle to keep it alive.

As Tiny Washington walked to the plate, swinging

his bat thoughtfully, Greer said, "Bet you five it's out of here."

"I never bet against my heart, Moose. You know that."

I liked Washington's chances against Grimes. He had doubled to lead off the second inning, but no one could score him. He had struck out since then.

He lined the third pitch into deep right field. I thought it was gone, as did most of the fans, but it hit the fence. Redmond caught it on one bounce for a double. Sloane went to third.

Orca Elliott was the lefthanded designated hitter. As he approached the plate, Marty Hogan came out of the first-base dugout to talk to Grimes and Dick Peel, the catcher. It was a brief conversation. When Peel got back behind the plate, he raised four fingers in the air, signalling the intentional walk.

"Playing the percentages," Glebe grunted. "He wants to pitch to the righthander."

Joe Kelsey was on deck, watching carefully as Grimes threw four balls outside the strike zone. Peel almost missed the last one, jumping a foot off the ground.

"I'd love to see Preacher park this one," I said. "Just so Thorson would have to thank him."

The din was unbelievable. Toronto fans are notorious for their quietness, but this crowd was something else. I could see normally staid people I knew in the crowd, standing and stamping and clapping, screaming themselves hoarse.

The first pitch was a called strike. The second was inside and high. The third was outside and low. The fourth was a terrible mistake, right where Kelsey wanted it, and he hit a ball that was gone the minute it left his bat, still rising when it went over the left-field fence.

And all the screaming stopped. There was an instant,

a heartbeat of silence when he hit it, a great collective gasp, followed immediately by noise that made what had gone before sound like a murmur, while Kelsey circled the bases.

I am a sucker for moments of triumph. I can watch Sunday afternoon bowling and get a lump in my throat when one lout from Des Moines beats another, so I was fairly unglued by Kelsey's home run. Embarrassed, I bent my head to my blurry keyboard and began to write.

Around me, the Boston writers were trashing Hogan for walking Elliott and the Toronto writers were wondering how Thorson planned to blow this lead. Moose looked at me, then winked.

On the field, Harry Grimes was impassive, The Titans who had mobbed Kelsey when he came off the field sat back down. To show their glee would be an uncalled-for slap in the ego for the Red Sox, but the excitement was obvious. They were chattering among themselves and most of them found reason to move around: to the water cooler for a drink, to the bat rack to check equipment, up the runway for a nervous pee.

Thorson sat almost out of sight in the corner of the dugout, with his jacket on his right arm. He crossed and uncrossed his legs, adjusted his jock and leaned forward, his elbows on his knees. When Swain grounded out to the first baseman, he got up, dropped his jacket, grabbed his glove, and ran to the mound, eager to get it over with.

Suddenly there was a shout from the back row of the press box. Sidney, Moose's assistant, was standing with a telephone held to his ear and a grin all over his face.

"Tommy Cole just hit a three-run homer. It's 5–3, Cleveland."

"What inning?" Greer asked.

"Bottom of the eighth."

"Don't hang up that phone."

Six outs to go. Thorson got the first three in a row, on a groundout to short, pop to third, and a strikeout. The crowd, still standing after Kelsey's home run, cheered every pitch. The celebrations had begun, and they were impatient for the game to end.

They kept cheering when Gloves Gardiner led off with a walk and Owl Wise followed with a single to short right. They booed when Marty Hogan trudged out of the visiting dugout to pull Harry Grimes from the game. He signalled, too late, for his ace reliever, Matt Harata, the Hawaiian lefthander with the 93-mile-an-hour fastball. After eight innings of Grimes's slow stuff, it would be hard for the hitters to adjust.

Sure enough, Eddie Carter grounded into a double play, but Jones scored Wise from third with a single to left. David Sloane struck out.

And Sidney hung up the phone with a bang.

"It's over! Indians won!"

"It's going to get weird out, real soon," said Jeff. "Look at the fans!"

As the Titans took the field for the ninth inning, the scoreboard flashed the score from Cleveland. Pandemonium. Security guards and policemen moved to the bottom of each aisle. They were as excited as anyone else, and when the fans shouted at them to get out of the way, they hunkered down, grinning.

Thorson's job wasn't easy. He had to face the meat of the Red Sox order, starting with Teddy Amaro, the number-two hitter. He hit a line drive right at Thorson, who made the catch in self-defence.

Young Randy Slaughter topped a grounder to Billy Wise, who flipped it to Tiny Washington. Two out. Bobby Johnson, who didn't want to be the last out, marched angrily to the plate, pumped up by the booing all around him.

73

When he hit the first pitch hard and high to left field, Preacher Kelsey fairly danced with joy at the chance to catch the ball. He did it exuberantly, but with both hands, then grabbed it and pumped it in the air as Gardiner and Thorson, who had both frozen to watch the catch, met halfway to the mound in an embrace, soon to be swamped by the rest of the players as the dugout emptied.

I put the binoculars on Preacher as he did some fancy broken-field running through the fans who were streaming onto the field. He lost his cap on the way but didn't let go of the ball, which he gave to Thorson.

Thorson put his arm around Kelsey's shoulder and then, surprisingly, handed the ball back. Then tears blurred my eyes again, and I got up and joined the rest of the reporters heading for the elevator.

Moose hugged me.

"Holy fuck. They did it."

We ran down the corridor to the clubhouse, with the sound of the stamping, shouting fans booming and echoing overhead. As I walked through the doors, I was hit by the first champagne shower. The sickeningly sweet Ontario bubbly stung my eyes terribly. When I could see again, Bony Costello was holding the now empty bottle and grinning, his own uniform soaked, his hair hanging in his eyes.

"Gotcha," he said, then hugged me and lifted me off my feet. It was like being mauled by a bear, but not altogether unpleasant. When he dropped me, I retrieved as much dignity as I could, given that I was drenched with wine, and set off in search of Joe Kelsey.

He was on the platform that had been set up by the NBC crew, waiting with Thorson and Ted Ferguson while Bert Nelson interviewed Red O'Brien. The other players watched, swigging champagne from the bottles and whooping with joy, already drunk with happiness.

Alex Jones had five bottles stashed at his locker. He opened them, one at a time, and made forays into the room to douse his teammates. When Nelson turned his microphone to Ferguson, it was Jones who jumped on the platform and christened the pair. I took snide satisfaction in watching Ferguson's expensive ultrasuede jacket soak up the wine.

There was no point in taking notes while they spouted platitudes on the stand. I went looking for comment from some of the lesser stars.

I found Gloves Gardiner sitting in front of his locker, tears streaming down his face.

"I've got twelve years in this game, and I've never even come close," he said. "I was afraid I never would."

"It was a great game."

"I'm so proud of all the guys. Steve was awesome."

"You and he almost got into it in the first inning. What was that about?"

"I was just reminding him that we are all in this together," Gardiner said, smiling tightly. "But that's all history now. Now we have to look ahead to the playoffs."

"What about the A's? Are you thinking about them yet?"

"Yeah, a bit. Oakland is a tough team, but we had a good record against them during the season, and in our division they would have finished fourth. This was the big one to win."

I could see that Kelsey was finished with the television interviews, so I left with Gloves and fought my way to Joe's locker.

There was such a mob I couldn't even see him or hear a word he said until Tiny Washington, at the next locker, pulled his stool out for me to stand on. I tried shouting questions, but it was no use. I stood on my perch and just watched for a moment.

Plastic sheets had been taped over all the lockers to protect the players' clothes. The clubhouse was as crowded as the Eaton's Boxing Day sale, a happy, jostling mass of players, reporters, and hangers-on.

Jones was still a one-man champagne raiding party. He was going nuts, a nineteen-year-old man-child in his glory. When he ran out of targets, he poured the stuff over his own head.

Flakey Patterson had found a Canadian flag and stood draped in it, babbling and eating, released from his vows. Thorson was in a corner, surrounded as completely as Kelsey, smiling and talking. Eddie Carter had a tape deck turned up to full volume and was boogying with Archie Griffin in a corner.

A couple of bat boys were sneaking drinks, looking around furtively. Goober Grabowski and Stinger Swain had lined up bottles in front of them for some competitive chugalugging.

Moose Greer, sweating profusely, came to the door and bellowed: "Cover up, guys, you got guests!" Then he ushered in the players' wives and girlfriends.

Jones, spying new victims, grabbed several bottles and ran across the room, and soon the women were soaking, too, carefully coiffed hair in rat-tails, mascara running down their cheeks. They found and embraced their husbands in the chaos.

"Pretty sight, isn't it?"

Startled, I turned and found that Joe Kelsey had climbed up next to me on his stool. He had neither wife nor girlfriend in town, but didn't seem to mind.

"You did it, Preacher," I said.

He turned to me, eyes wet, and said, "I did it, Kate."

We shook hands solemnly, then laughed. I leaned over and kissed him on the cheek and he hugged me, hard.

"He gave you the ball?"

"You saw that? Wasn't that something?"

"You both deserved it, today."

Just then, Moose shouted to Kelsey from the door-way. "The man who caught your home-run ball is out-side. He wants you to sign it for him."

"I'll do better than that!"

He grabbed a bat and went to the door. He was back a moment later, with the ball in his hand.

"I traded him," Kelsey said, "for a bat and a pair of tickets to the first playoff game."

Then he walked across the room to Thorson's locker. I couldn't hear what he said when he handed it to him, but I could see their faces. They were serious, as though making a pledge. Then they embraced.

Oh, shit. It set me off again. I hopped down from the stool and began to make the rounds, happy as Elwy in a bowl of cream. I found Jeff, and we split up the team, making sure we got quotes from everybody. I started off with Thorson, fighting my way through the crowd.

"What did you have to say to Kelsey after the game, Steve?"

"Jesus Christ, woman, don't you ever let up? I just pitched the team into the playoffs and you want to know what I said to Kelsey? Get off my case."

He turned away from me and kept on answering questions.

"Charming," said Christopher Morris.

"A real prince of a guy," I agreed.

"QUIET!"

Moose's voice cut through the babble.

"Can I have your attention, please? The clubhouse is now closed. We ask all players to please stand by for a meeting, wives and girlfriends to go back to the lounge, and all members of the media to assemble immediately in the board room for a press conference."

There was a general murmur of confusion and protest, but one look at Moose's face was enough to convince most of us that something serious was up.

Ted Ferguson was waiting for us, looking uncomfortable. As soon as we were settled, he told Moose to close the door.

"I regret to have to inform you that Pedro Jorge Sanchez was found dead in his condominium at approximately 3:45 this afternoon." The announcement was formal and chilling.

"What happened?"

Drugs? Heart attack?

"The cause of death won't be official until the autopsy is complete, but it appears that he died during a robbery."

"When did it happen?"

"Probably sometime last night."

"Who found him?"

"When he hadn't appeared by game time, and there was no reply to repeated telephone calls, one of our staff went to see if he was all right. The superintendent of the building provided a key and the two discovered his body. The police were then called to the scene."

"Was he shot, or what?"

"We don't have any details."

"Who is in charge of the investigation?"

Ferguson checked a notepad in front of him.

"Staff Sergeant Lloyd Munro, of the homicide squad, has been assigned to the case."

"What about his wife? Does she know?"

"We're still trying to reach her in Santo Domingo."

There was an uneasy silence. Finally, I asked the cold, but inevitable, question.

"What does this do to the rest of the season?"

"We don't know. Red is telling the players now, and I expect they will come to a decision about continuing or not. Tomorrow is an off day, as you know, so they'll be able to think about it overnight.

"Moose will keep you informed, and we'll have some sort of press conference tomorrow. And that's really all I have to say. If you'll excuse me, I must go talk with the players."

When Ferguson left, everyone began to talk at once. Murders were not the normal stuff of our professional lives. I hadn't covered a crime since I was a junior reporter fifteen years before. I'd hated it.

I called Jake Watson from the phone in Moose's office and told him what I knew.

"It just came over the wire," he said. "I've checked with city side. Jimmy Peterson's working on it. I'll get you transferred."

Peterson is the cop reporter, an ancient, old-fashioned guy who has held down the beat for thirty-five years and has better connections on the force than the chief.

"Peterson." His voice was gruff and impatient, but that's just his style. He always sounds as if he's got a fedora on the back of his head, with a press pass stuck in the band. He still smokes cigars, no matter what rules the newsroom tight-asses try to enforce.

"Jimmy, it's Kate Henry. I'm at the Titan offices. We've just heard about the Sultan Sanchez murder. What do you know?"

"Beaten to death. The proverbial blunt instrument. The place was a mess. Looks like he interrupted a burglar."

"Who's this guy who's in charge of the investigation? Lloyd Munro? I haven't heard of him before."

"He's good. Young. Smart. He's a little unconventional but gets away with it because he's Donald Munro's son. Head of homicide in the fifties. Killed on duty. Before your time."

"What's he like to deal with?"

"Tough. Doesn't like the press. He'll talk to me. I knew his dad. Don't know about you. He's at Fifty-two Division."

He gave me the number and I asked him to transfer me back to the sports desk. He didn't say good-bye. In a moment, Jake came back on the line.

"Jimmy'll do the murder. You get reaction down there from the players and cover the baseball angle. What's going to happen with the rest of the season?"

"The players are meeting right now. I'll stake out the dressing room and get back to you as soon as I know anything." Moose came into the office as I hung up.

"What else do you know? What staff member found him?"

"It was Jocelyn. She's freaked out. You can't talk to her."

Jocelyn Mah was Moose's secretary. Poor kid.

"Where is she?"

"She left. The cops told her not to talk to anyone."

"Right. What's the word from the players?"

"They're still in the meeting."

"I'll go wait in the hall. See you."

"Wait. Do you want to get some dinner after?"

"I don't know when I'll be through, Moose."

"I thought I'd go to the Fillet around nine."

"I'll see. If I'm done, maybe I'll meet you there."

I went out into the corridor under the stands. An equipment truck was coming from the Red Sox dressing room, followed by a few players on the way to catch the team bus to the airport. Teddy Amaro stopped when he saw me.

"It it true about Pedro?"

The two had once been teammates, in Cincinnati.

"I'm sorry, Teddy. I'm afraid so."

I filled him in on the few details I knew until the

Red Sox travelling secretary shouted at him that the bus was about to go. He thanked me and ran to catch up.

Down the corridor to the left, the stakeout was on. A dozen or more reporters leaned against the wall outside the Titan clubhouse door. There were three film crews. I went the other way, towards the visiting clubhouse. There was an unmarked doorway halfway around the curving corridor. I knocked on it.

Karin Gardiner let me in to the players' families lounge. A dozen women sat around the room in silence, while the children played with toys on the floor. A couple were fighting, another couple crying, comforted by their mothers.

"What's she doing here? No press allowed." It was Dummy Doran's wife, a former Las Vegas showgirl. She wore a fur jacket over tight blue jeans and stiletto-heeled boots.

"Maybe Kate can tell us what's happening, Helene." Karin said. "What's the meeting about? Something about Sultan? He's dead?"

"Yes. He's been murdered."

Sandi Thorson stood up, her hand to her mouth, took two steps towards me, and fainted.

There was a great commotion. More children began to cry. Wives gathered around her, ineffectually patting her wrists and cheeks, like they do in the movies.

"Step back, for God's sake," said Helene Doran. She kneeled at Sandi's head, loosened her shirt, and lifted her head.

"Get me my bag," she said, pointing a scarlet fingernail. "There's a flask inside."

I found it and brought it to her.

"Hurry up. Pour some, don't be stupid," she said.

I poured an inch of what seemed to be vodka into the silver cap. Helene forced it between Sandi's lips.

She coughed and came around. Imagine that. Just like in the movies.

"I'm sorry," she said, getting up.

Steve, Junior, her two-year-old, put his arms around her knees. She sat down and took him onto her lap. He stuck his thumb into his mouth and leaned his head against her breast.

"Please," she said. "Tell us how it happened."

I told the story, watching for reaction. Most showed shock, horror, all sorts of appropriate emotions, but there were a few who didn't. Helene Doran looked bored. Mary Mason, the wife of Josh Mason, the back-up catcher, looked somehow triumphant.

"He was a devil," she said, vehemently. "He was punished for his sins."

The Masons were the King and Queen of Born-Agains on the team, and she was pretty hardline, but I was still surprised. Other wives nodded in agreement; Marie Sloane and Sandi Thorson were still stunned.

"Wait a minute," said Darlene Washington. "No matter how evil he was, and he was plenty evil, it's a horrible way to die. Poor Dolores. And his children."

Trust Darlene to be as level-headed as her husband. I left them then and headed back towards the clubhouse. The meeting was letting out. I took down a few quotes from the shocked players, then waylaid Gloves.

"What's going to happen now?"

"We'll get together again late tomorrow afternoon to decide. Red figured that everybody needs the day off to think about it. Between you and me, I think we'll play."

It made sense. With the division clinched, they could take the rest of the week off in mourning and go straight into the playoffs, but it wouldn't feel right. They'd cloak it in "Sultan would have wanted it this way" clichés, but most of them were probably thinking about their performance bonuses. Besides, they didn't want an asterisk by their win.

That was too cold, maybe. Maybe it was just that the best way for them to deal with Sanchez's death was to throw themselves into their work. Their work just happened to be play for most people.

10

I went back to the office to work. That was my first mistake. Everyone from the managing editor to the copy boys wanted to talk about the murder while I tried to write a game story, a sidebar about the celebrations, a story about the Titan reaction to Sanchez's death, and help with the obituary. Four pages of the sports section were being devoted to the peculiar combination of triumph and tragedy.

I also talked to Dolores Sanchez, in Santo Domingo, and put the junior reporter on the trail of Jocelyn Mah. There were 113 Mahs in the phone book, but he managed to find the right house. Her father wouldn't let me speak to her, but assured me that she wouldn't be talking to anyone else.

I also called Staff Sergeant Munro. When he hadn't called back by ten, I left the number at the Fillet of Soul with the desk and called it a night.

Moose was there when I got to the restaurant, sitting at the Jeffersons' table with Sarah. A moment later, Tom came over from the bar, carrying a very large martini.

"You look like you could use this," he said.

"It will either fix me up or finish me off," I said, toasting him.

"What a day," Moose said. He had obviously had a few already. His eyes were in soft focus.

"Any news?"

"Nothing."

"When did you close up shop?"

"I didn't get out of there until nearly nine."

"What about the rest?"

"Don't know."

"I talked to Dolores Sanchez. She's flying up tomorrow."

"Christ, that's all I need."

"Moose!"

"Sorry, Sarah. But you try getting everything ready for the playoffs, then throw in a murder just to make things really ugly. Pressure? It's ridiculous."

"Maybe we'd better get some food, Sarah. I could use it, and I'm sure Moose could. Steak okay, big guy?"

"Yeah, okay. Well done. And another double bourbon."

"I'll have mine rare with a glass of red wine, please."

Sarah went to place the order.

"Are you okay, Moose? You look whipped."

"I'll be okay after another drink."

"Maybe you should take it easy. Are you going to able to handle everything without Jocelyn?"

"I don't know how I'm going to get the playoff credentials done in time."

"Isn't the Baseball Writers' Association helping you?"

"Yeah, sure. All Stan Chapman cares about is making sure his friends get good seats in the press box."

"If you like, I can come in and give you a hand for a while tomorrow. I know who the legitimate writers are."

"No, I can handle it. But thanks."

I'd known Moose for a long time and liked him. He could be a boor, but most of his insensitivity stemmed from insecurity. His was a funny, drifting sort of life. Most men in their forties have something to show for it, but Moose's only history was of failure. He didn't have much education and no real skills. He'd gone from high school into baseball and never been more than a marginal major-leaguer. He hadn't made much money, and what he'd made he'd spent.

He'd been married, but his wife had taken the children and gone just after he was released from his last team. He had a few rocky years then, bitter, boozing times, until Ted Ferguson heard he was down on his luck and hired him. Baseball was all he knew, and he was lucky to have his job.

Ironically, the Titan players didn't see him as one of them. He was too old and insignificant for most of the current crop to have heard of. In July, the Titan visit to Milwaukee had coincided with an Old-Timers' game and Moose had suited up with the Brewer alumni. He was happier that afternoon than he had been all season.

I looked at his hands. They showed the scars. He had been a catcher, and his fingers were misshapen, with bulging knuckles and tips bending off in unlikely directions where they had been broken. His soul probably looked the same. Moose was all the baseball dreams that never come true.

God, I was getting sentimental.

"I'll drive you home after dinner, Moose. You're in no condition."

"What are you, my mother? Did anyone ever tell you you're a pain in the ass?"

Sarah came back in time to hear the last remark and raised her eyebrows at me as she sat down.

"This should be a happy night," she said. "This place should be jumping, but look at everybody. They're in shock."

Dinner didn't help Moose. He was bagged by the time he was done, and getting belligerent. I decided to take him home.

"Come back when you've dropped him off," Sarah said.

The fresh air seemed to have an aphrodisiac effect. He began to paw me as soon as we got in the car.

"Whoa, Moose. That's not a good idea."

"C'mon Katey. F'r old time's sake."

We had had a brief fling three years earlier, born out of loneliness on a particularly long road trip, but it had ended as soon as we got home. I didn't intend to start again.

"For old time's sake, Moose, let's keep it friendly." He looked at me earnestly.

"I'm being friendly, Katey. This is friendly."

I took his hand out from under my skirt and headed up Yonge Street. It was wild. A lot of people either hadn't heard about Sultan or didn't care. The drunks were all over the street, dancing and shouting while the cops looked on.

I bailed out as soon as I could and headed up University. Things were quieter on the pretentious avenue. I stopped at a light next to the Airmen's memorial, the one we call Gumby Takes Flying Lessons.

"Hey, Gumby! What's happenin'?"

It was his last outburst. Perhaps he passed out, because he was quiet when we went around Queen's Park, the provincial legislature building, which would have been a noble thing if it wasn't so awfully pink.

He lived in an apartment building on St. George, north of the Medical Centre. When I pulled up in front, he was snoring. I got out and walked around to open his door.

"Come on, Moose. We're home."

"'S'okay. I'm gonna sleep here."

"Moose. You're in a car. A tiny car. You'll wake up like a pretzel."

"Don' wanna pretzel. Wanna sleep."

I got the giggles. There was no doorman to help me. The street was deserted, all good Torontonians having gone to bed early to get ready for Monday morning. The rest were on Yonge Street, hanging off the lampposts. I pulled on his arm.

"Wake up, Moose. Time for beddy bye."

He opened his eyes and focused them, approximately, on me. He smiled and reached out his arms. I ducked the clumsy embrace and took both his hands.

"Let's go, Moose. Upsy daisy."

Oh, he was going to owe me for this. He outweighed me by a hundred pounds, so I couldn't carry him, but I pulled as hard as I could, cajoling him all the way. He finally got out of the car and stood, swaying alarmingly. I reached into his pocket for his keys, then guided him to the door.

"Which key, Moose?"

"Key of C," he said, then began to sing, loudly, the Titan theme song.

I propped him against the mailboxes and got the lobby door open, then steered him to the elevator. At the 10th floor, I leaned him again and got the door to his apartment opened.

"Home, sweet home," he said, stumbling into the living room. "How about a little cocktail?"

"Moose. Sit down."

I left him sprawled on the couch in his messy living room. The apartment had been done by a decorator from

the *Playboy* school, with thick broadloom, leather fur-
niture, and state-of-the-art sound and video equipment.
The bedroom was red, with a fur rug on the king-sized
bed. The hallway was lined with pictures of Moose as
a player and ones posed with Hall of Fame stars he'd
met through his Titan job. But everything was a bit tired
looking. The swinging bachelor pad didn't look like it
got much use.

In the bathroom, the clothes hamper was overflow-
ing and whiskers stuck to the sides of the sink. There
was a scummy grey ring around the black Jacuzzi. A
torn shirt hung on the doorknob and there were soggy
towels on the floor. I found a large bottle of 222's in
the medicine cabinet and a cleanish glass on the counter.

"You'll thank me for this in the morning," I said,
coming into the living room with the water and two
pills. Moose was on his feet again, trying to cram a
handful of papers into an already full drawer.

"Don't bother tidying. I'm not staying. You just get
to bed. I'll phone you in the morning."

He looked confused. I put the glass in his right hand,
the pills in his left, and kissed him on the cheek.

"Your keys are on the desk. Your car is at the Fillet.
Sleep well."

He was heading towards the bar, muttering to himself, when I closed the door.

I was back at the restaurant just before one a.m. The
front door was locked, so I went around to the kitchen
and knocked loudly.

Tom answered, a glass of champagne in his hand.

"Come on in. We locked the door to keep strangers
out."

In the bar a few regulars were holding a low-key
celebration. Tom gave me a glass, and we toasted the
Titans.

We talked until five in the morning about the old

days, about players, now out of baseball, who had spent time in Toronto. We toasted them, too. We wallowed in history while the newly minted fans who couldn't tell you the starting lineup for the playoffs were tearing up the town.

The phone by my bed rang at nine. I knocked it on the floor, then put it to my ear upside down. When I finally got it right and croaked a greeting, it was Moose, sounding cheerier than he had any right to be.

"You're full of shit," I groaned. "I know you don't feel as good as you sound."

"Kate! Top of the morning to you. It's a beautiful day. Why shouldn't I feel good?"

"You were a bit rocky last night."

"That's what I was calling about. We were together, right?"

"Approximately."

"Do you know where I parked my car?"

Smugly, I told him.

"Thanks. And I'll tell you the truth. I feel terrible. I hope I didn't get out of line."

"No problem, Moose. But you owe me one."

"You got it."

I felt horrible. I stumbled to the bathroom and popped

a couple of 222's, then went to put on the kettle. I gagged dishing out Elwy's food. He dug right in.

I was on my way to the shower when Sally appeared.

"How are you, kiddo?"

"Don't ask."

"Have you got the kettle on? I just got T.C. off to school. He's freaked about Sultan Sanchez."

"Come on in. How come you're not at work?"

"I have to work late. I'm not going in until noon. Are you home tonight?"

"Should be, why?"

"If you wouldn't mind keeping an ear open for the kid until I get home."

"No problem. Do you want me to give him supper?"

"No, I've left it for him."

"I'll be home by six at the latest. He can come watch TV with me. There's a Yankee game on."

"As long as he's in bed by nine-thirty."

"Yes, ma'am."

Sally's gallery was opening a new show that night. She was telling me about some of the bizarre images when the phone rang again. This time it was Jake Watson.

"It's still early, Jake. What can't wait?"

"Murder can't wait, Kate."

"Moose is going to call me here to tell me when the press conference is. I'll cover it."

"*Another* murder."

"Not another player?"

"Steve Thorson."

"What? When? Where?"

I was beginning to sound like a journalism textbook.

"Last night. At the ballpark."

"The ballpark?"

"In the clubhouse. Beaten to death."

"Oh, no." I sat down. Sally looked at me and passed my cigarettes. I lit one.

"What do we know?"

"Not much. Just what Jimmy Peterson got from the cops. One of the clubhouse kids found the body. I want you to get down to the stadium and see what you can get for the final edition."

"I'll be there in twenty minutes."

So much for my shower. I threw on some clothes, pulled a brush through my tangled hair, and hit the road without even stopping to put on makeup. I looked like a bag lady.

I'd left my car at the Fillet so I took a cab, my eyes in slits against the sun despite dark glasses. I could taste my sour stomach. I was so hung over my hair hurt.

There were a couple of police cruisers in the stadium parking lot. I went around to the Titan office entrance. Not giving her a chance to stop me, I waved at the receptionist on my way through the inner door. I went straight to Moose's office, which was empty. I asked a secretary where he was.

"He's in the clubhouse with the police, but I don't think you should go in there."

"I'll let them tell me that, thanks."

There was an ambulance at the door to the Titan dressing room, with a policeman standing guard. His back was to me. I ducked down the umpires' tunnel to the field and peeked into the end of the dugout. There was nobody guarding that door. I was torn between getting the hell out of there before I was discovered and pressing on to get as much of a story as I could.

The clubhouse door opened and I ducked back into the tunnel. I heard a single set of footsteps and then silence.

I peeked out and saw a teenaged boy in jeans, sweatshirt, and windbreaker with a Titan logo. I knew him only as Craig. He was one of the clubhouse attendants who kept the place clean, washed the uniforms, cleaned the spikes, and generally kept the players happy. Craig was the wise-ass in the group, always cool, but this morning he looked very young, very pale, and very scared. He was slumped against a corner of the dugout, staring at the field, trying not to cry.

I whispered his name urgently, and he jumped.

"Sorry," I said quietly, crossing the dugout to sit next to him. "How are you doing?"

"Did you hear what happened?" He was whispering, too.

"Yeah. Feel like telling me about it?"

"I don't think you're supposed to be here."

"I'm probably not. But I thought you might want to talk about it. It must have been pretty tough for you."

Craig looked at me, then back at the field, his lips in a tight line. I put my arm around his shoulders.

"It's okay to be upset," I said.

Then the tears came, and the great, tearing sobs. I held him tightly until he got himself under control, shushing him and stroking his bristly crewcut. After a few minutes he straightened up, wiping his eyes with the back of his tanned hand. I gave him a tissue from my purse. He was embarrassed.

"No shame in tears, Craig," I said.

"Thanks," he said, his dignity restored. "It was really awful. There was all this blood on the floor, and I could see his brains. It was so gross."

"How come you were the only one here?"

"They said we could go home last night without cleaning up, but we had to be in at nine. I got a ride downtown with my dad, so I got here early."

"How did you get in?"

"Ravi, the security guy, let me in."

"What happened?"

"When I got in the dressing room I heard one of the

showers dripping. So I went in to turn it off and he was there."

The boy shuddered and looked at me, tears in his eyes again. He took a deep breath and continued.

"He was sort of curled up on the floor. At first I thought he was asleep. So I go, 'Hey, Steve, didn't you make it home last night?' but he didn't move. So I went over and took him by the shoulder. I was going to shake him. But he felt real funny and kind of rolled over a bit. Then I saw his face and I just ran away. I guess I got sick, too."

"What did you see?"

"His forehead was like bashed in. There was all the blood, and his eyes were open. I just left him there and went and got Ravi. He called 911."

Craig had started to shake, and I took his hand. I didn't really know what to say. I checked my watch to see how I was doing on my deadline. Nice, eh?

"Don't worry, Craig. I'll just wait with you here until they call you."

"Won't you get in trouble?"

"What can they do, arrest me?"

I wasn't sure what kind of trouble I could get into, but I figured that at worst they would toss me out of the stadium. And I would still have my story.

We sat in silence for a few minutes. Then Craig spoke.

"Miss Henry? Who do you think did it?"

"I don't know, Craig."

"Do you think it's someone we know?"

It was hard to imagine a stranger getting into the clubhouse. But it was harder to imagine, as Craig said, someone we knew bashing his head in. This train of thought only served to remind me of the state of my own head.

97

I let go of Craig's hand and went to the water fountain to take a couple more headache pills. As I was straightening up, the clubhouse door opened.

It was a young police constable, in uniform, who looked from Craig to me thoughtfully. Craig looked scared again. I wiped the water off my chin.

"You can come in, Craig," said the constable. "They're ready to talk to you now. But will you ask Staff Sergeant Munro to come out here first?"

I did my best to look inconspicuous as the kid went inside. It didn't work. The cop walked towards me, hand resting on his billy club. He was huge.

"Hi," I said. "I was just trying to calm Craig down. He was pretty upset."

"Who are you, and how did you get here?" he asked, sternly. He was so young that I had trouble taking him seriously. He looked like a high school actor playing a cop in the school play. Another sign of middle age. I tried to stare him down.

"I'm Katherine Henry, and I got here through the umpires' tunnel," I said. "I am a baseball writer for the *Planet*."

"But how did you get into the stadium?"

"Through the Titan offices," I said. "Is there any reason I shouldn't be here?"

"This is a crime scene, Miss. You'll have to talk to Staff Sergeant Munro."

On cue, the door opened. The man who came out looked as much like a cop as I look like Dolly Parton. He wasn't big, he wasn't beefy, and he wasn't wearing polyester. He was slim and elegant, dressed in what looked like a good silk tweed jacket and pants with a fashionable pleat. His tie was loosened slightly and the jacket undone. I could see his gun.

He ran his fingers through his dark, wavy hair.

"What's up, MacPherson?"

"I found this lady attempting to interfere with the witness, sir," the constable said. "She's a reporter."

"You make it sound as if I was molesting him, for heaven's sake. I was just trying to comfort him. He was almost in shock, in case you hadn't noticed."

Amusement flashed in Munro's eyes briefly, then he turned to his young colleague.

"Thanks for your vigilance, Constable," he said, dismissing him. Then he turned to me.

"You're Katherine Henry, aren't you? I've seen your picture in the paper. I'm pleased to meet you."

A bit taken aback, I shook his hand.

"I'm just as glad you're here. I can't tell you much for the record, but maybe you can tell me some things. You knew Thorson and the rest of the Titans well. I'd like to ask you some informal questions, if you don't mind."

"I'll do anything I can, but I have to get something back to my paper. When are you releasing information?"

"Not until we know more ourselves."

"Are you sure it couldn't have been an accident?"

"Not the way his skull was broken. There's nothing in the shower room that could have caused that kind of injury if he fell. Also some other things I can't talk about. There's no chance he wasn't murdered."

"Do you think it's connected to Sultan Sanchez's death?"

"It certainly puts a new light on it. You know all the people around the team. Do you have any idea of who might want to kill either one of them?"

"Couldn't Thorson's killer have been a stranger, too? Maybe it's just a coincidence."

"We don't believe much in coincidences where I work."

"It's crazy. Who would want to kill Thorson? Thorson had enemies, but not murderous ones. Some of his

teammates didn't like him, and guys on other teams, but baseball players don't go around killing people."

I realized I was babbling and shut up.

"I thought Thorson was the biggest star on the team," Munro said. "He wasn't popular?"

"Well, the fans liked him, and he was still one of their best pitchers, but he wasn't the nicest guy. But that's no reason to kill him."

"Were you in the dressing room after the game yesterday?"

"Yes, of course. Why?"

"Well, after we talk, maybe you could have a look around and see if anything seems out of the ordinary now."

I didn't want to go in there. But I couldn't pass up the chance.

"I guess," I said. "Is he, is it, still there?"

"No, no. The body has been removed. Would you mind?"

He held open the door, then stopped.

"Do you know if this lock is usually taped like this?"

The door was one of a pair of self-locking steel doors with a bar to open them from inside. Where the lock met the latchplate in the matching door, there was a torn scrap of adhesive tape.

"It looks as if the lock was taped to let someone get in here without a key," I said. "I don't know if it was like this yesterday or not. But a couple of times I've tried to get in this way after a game or when I arrive really early and it's been locked."

Munro grunted. Approvingly, I guess.

"Good," he said. "You're observant. You might be some use after all. We've already taken samples. It appears to be the kind of tape they use on bats."

The clubhouse was actually a complex of rooms off a zigzagging central corridor. Just past the dugout

entrance was a washroom for players to use during a game. Around the corner was the equipment room. The bats and gloves were all over the floor.

Around the next corner was the main player area, with the trainer's room on one side of the corridor, the main dressing room on the other. I looked in as we passed. Instead of players and reporters, there were half a dozen men in suits. Instead of television crews, there was a police photographer. Instead of hilarity and celebration, there was the slow, sober work of observation, the beginning stages of the investigation.

Munro and I continued around the next corner, past the manager's office, where his colleague was questioning Craig, to the players' lounge. Someone had fired up the coffee machine, and Munro poured two cups. He handed one to me and we sat facing each other diagonally from two couches in a corner of the room.

"What connection was there between Thorson and Sanchez?"

"I can't think of anything except the obvious. They didn't have much to do with each other. I can't imagine that they would have seen each other off the field except at team functions or charity appearances. They didn't have much in common."

Munro nodded, taking notes in a spiral-bound book. The affability was gone. Now he was at work. I wasn't used to being on this side of an interview and didn't like it much.

"There are factions on the team, then?"

"Well, the Latin players tend to stick together, probably more for language than anything else. Blacks tend to be close to blacks, whites to whites. The religious group crosses race and language lines. The older players hang out with each other, as do the rookies. But there isn't hostility among the various groups, so they aren't factions in that sense."

"Who were Thorson's close friends?"

"No one on the team. He was a star. Some players were in awe of him, others resented him. He was a loner. He wasn't part of the clubhouse practical jokes or anything.

"I guess you could say that the other players tolerated him, but he wasn't really liked. Except for Archie Griffin, the rookie. He liked him. But he likes everyone."

"Who were his enemies, then?"

"I'm not saying he had enemies, just no close friends. Don't put words into my mouth."

"But there must have been some who had more reason to dislike him than others."

I didn't really like where this was taking us. Inevitably, I was going to cast suspicion on one of the players, and I wasn't in any position to do that. Besides, I couldn't believe any of them could have done it.

"Look, there were a lot of guys who didn't like him, but these men aren't criminals. Some of the fielders had a problem with him, for example, because he would blame them for his losses but give them no credit when he won.

"Others resented how easily success came to him. These would be the ones who had to struggle to make it to the big leagues and to hang on once they got here.

"The manager didn't like him because Thorson was a pipeline to Ted Ferguson, the owner. I could go on through the whole team and give you reasons. Hell, the clubhouse kids didn't like him because he was a lousy tipper. But none of this adds up to a motive for murder."

"I might be the best judge of that," Munro said. "What about people outside the team?"

Like his agent. I couldn't believe that I had forgotten about Craven. I told Munro about my conversation with Morris, stressing that all I had was gossip and speculation. Then it was my turn to ask questions.

"When do you think he was killed?"

"It's hard to pin it down yet. The coroner could only say that it was sometime in the last twelve hours. So it could have happened any time during the night. Probably earlier rather than later. We'll know better after the autopsy."

He closed his notebook and stood up.

"You've been very helpful. Are you ready for the dressing room?"

I butted my cigarette and stood up.

"As ready as I'll ever be."

12

The Titan dressing room was a mess. Socks and jock straps lay in soggy little heaps on the floor. The plastic sheets on the lockers hung askew, partially torn from their thumbtacks. The television platforms were still up.

There were champagne and beer bottles everywhere: on the floor, in the garbage cans, propped on the tops of lockers. There was even a full one inside a cowboy boot in front of Swain's locker. He must have gone home in his shower slippers. The room reeked of sweat and sweet wine.

Yellow tape outlined a path through the dressing room to the showers. In rest of the room, half a dozen men were picking through the debris, taking photographs and looking for clues in the chaos. The whole place was filthy with black fingerprint powder. I didn't envy them their work.

"You've got an impossible job here," I said. "There must be 150 people who had a legitimate reason to leave fingerprints here yesterday afternoon alone."

"That many?" Munro looked alarmed.

"There are twenty-nine players on the roster. Add four coaches and the manager, the trainer, his assistant, the equipment manager, half a dozen bat boys and clubhouse kids. The ground crew. Security staff. There must have been sixty reporters and television people here before or after the game. The owner, the public relations director and other front-office people, and even the players' wives and girlfriends. It was a mob scene."

Munro looked gloomier by the minute. He ran his right hand through his hair again as he looked around the room.

"What time did you leave yesterday afternoon? Was Thorson still here?"

"Yes. There was a clubhouse meeting about Sanchez. The game ended just before four. I was here from about ten minutes after that until the meeting started, which must have been at four-thirty. Then there was a press conference after which I talked to the wives and waited for the players' meeting to be over. I guess I got back to the office at about five-thirty."

"How did the players react to the news?"

"They were shocked, of course, but they were mainly talking about whether they would play the rest of the season. They decided to wait until today to make the decision."

"And Thorson?"

"I didn't notice anything in particular. But his wife fainted when I told her."

"I wonder what that was about," he said.

"I've heard she's pregnant."

"Are there any problems in the marriage?"

"Not that I know of, but I wouldn't necessarily know. He screwed around a bit on the road. I don't know whether she knew about it or, for that matter, cared.

Athletes have pretty strange relationships with their wives. They're not like real people. Or not any people I know. They live in a time warp, stuck in the fifties when Daddy worked and Mummy stayed at home. I sure couldn't be married to one of them."

Munro allowed himself a small smile.

"What was Thorson like after the game yesterday?"

"He was part of all the euphoria. He wasn't right in the middle of things, but he was here, and he seemed to be enjoying himself. It was his finest moment, and he was milking everything he could out of it. The only one he had any harsh words with was me, come to think of it. Does that make me a suspect?"

"Just don't leave town, lady," he said, but he was still smiling. He looked tired. I felt sorry for him.

"If we're through, I'd better write my story. If I think of anything else, I'll let you know."

We exchanged business cards, and I started out the door. In the hall, I ran into Moose. He looked awful. His face was pale and blotchy, his eyes bloodshot.

"What are you doing here? I've been leaving messages for you everywhere. We've got a press briefing in the board room. The rest of the guys are there already. Five minutes."

He brushed past me and went to talk to Munro. I phoned Jake from the pay phone in the lounge. They had cobbled a story together on the police desk, so I dictated a few paragraphs about Craig and told him I'd try to get some more for the final edition. Jake said they'd hold it until twelve-thirty.

The board room was packed. Reporters sat in all the available chairs and there were television cameras and lights in place. I scrunched past two crews and found a spot to sit, nodding at the shocked familiar faces.

This was not a situation in which any of us felt comfortable, and we didn't know how best to handle it. We are the bearers of good tidings, usually, nothing more tragic than a demotion to the minor leagues or a couple of weeks on the disabled list. We deal in fantasy, in myth and symbolism, escape from the daily harsh realities and murder most foul.

The low murmur of voices stopped when Moose and Munro came in. Moose began the proceedings.

"As you all know by now, there has been a second murder. Titan pitcher Steve Thorson was found dead in the clubhouse a few hours ago."

He paused, looked down, and took a deep breath. Moose was as uncomfortable as the rest of us. Munro was the only one who looked relaxed.

"Staff Sergeant Lloyd Munro is in charge of the investigation, and he is here to answer any questions you might have. I'll tell you anything I can from the Titan angle. Staff Sergeant Munro?"

Munro had done up his tie and buttoned his jacket in honour of the cameras. He stood.

"Sometime last night or early this morning, Steve Thorson was apparently assaulted with a baseball bat in or near the shower room in the Titan clubhouse. His body was found at approximately eight-thirty this morning by Craig Murphy, age fifteen, one of the clubhouse attendants. At this time we have no suspects in custody."

"Does it look like an inside job?"

"Yes, we are operating on the assumption that the perpetrator was someone familiar with the layout of the stadium."

"You mean you suspect one of the players?"

"Not necessarily. It could have been a member of the organization, other stadium staff – even a member of the media." Munro stifled a small smile. "There are many possibilities, all of which are being investigated."

108

"Do you think there is a connection with Sultan Sanchez's murder?"

"If there isn't, it's one hell of a coincidence."

"Moose, what about tomorrow's game?"

"We don't know yet. Ted Ferguson is talking to the league office in New York. We're scheduled to play the Tigers and Yankees this week, and they're in a fight for second place, so the games are important for them."

"Have the players been contacted?"

"Red and the coaches have been on the phones all morning. The players will be meeting here at eleven, and those who wish to speak to the media will be available immediately afterwards. We've opened the press box for you to work in. The clubhouse is, for obvious reasons, closed."

"What about Thorson's family?"

"His wife, Sandi, was told immediately. Her parents were already in town, and his parents are scheduled to arrive this morning. We have representatives at the airport to meet them. Also, Dolores Sanchez. Of course, the organization will do anything we can to help both families."

Moose's clichés echoed dully in my ears. Some of the reporters asked for up-to-date statistics for Sanchez and Thorson, giving new meaning to the phrase "lifetime stats." They asked if the Titans would be wearing black armbands when they took the field.

This was getting me nowhere. It was getting close to eleven, so I decided to slip out and see if I could catch any of the players before they went into the meeting.

There were policemen guarding all the doors: the umpires' tunnel, the Titan offices, even the visiting clubhouse. There was no way to get on the field. I went down the corridor to the team parking lot.

I recognized Stinger Swain's silver Corvette and

Flakey Patterson's beat-up old Jeep. As I stood there, Tiny Washington pulled up in his white Cadillac with Joe Kelsey, Eddie Carter, and Slider Holmes, a rookie recently called up from the minors.

We all shook hands, made strangely formal by the circumstances. They were dressed somberly in dark suits and ties.

"Tell me what you know," Tiny said.

I told him about Craig, and about Staff Sergeant Munro.

"The poor kid," Joe said. "What an awful thing."

"So what are you going to do," I asked. "Are you going to play, or what?"

"That's what we're here to decide," Washington said. "We were talking about it on the way over, and we want to go ahead. It's all we know how. We'll dedicate the playoff series to Steve and Sultan and get on with it."

"I think they'd do the same," Kelsey said.

"Are you kidding," said Carter, bitterly. "They wouldn't think twice. Not with a World Series ring on the line."

Washington looked aggrieved.

"Cut that out, man," he said. "All's it's going to do is get you in trouble. Even if you are right."

They went inside the stadium. I waited in the parking lot and managed to talk to a dozen players. All were shocked and confused, but most were ready to play. I took the elevator to the press box and called Jake again.

"The players are in their meeting now, but it sounds as if they'll vote to play. Do you have room for a short sidebar?"

"Yeah, go for it. I'd like you to stay down there today and keep tabs on what's going on. I'll talk to you in an hour. Don't be late."

Moose came into the press box to announce that

another press conference was about to begin. Red O'Brien and David Sloane, the player representative, had statements to make. I went back downstairs.

There were no surprises. The players had decided to finish the season as originally scheduled. Sloane explained:

"We are shocked and saddened to lose our teammates Steve Thorson and Pedro Sanchez, and we intend no disrespect. We feel the only way to honour their memory is to win the World Series. They both would have wanted it this way."

And, yes, the players would be wearing black armbands. Sloane closed his remarks with a prayer.

Afterwards, Red announced that the league president had given the team permission to add two players to the playoff roster. He was bringing up Harry Belcher, a righthanded starter for the Titan Triple A club in Edmonton. Belcher would arrive later that night. Slider Holmes, who had not been eligible for the playoffs, would take Sanchez's spot on the roster.

I raised my hand.

"Moose, have any funeral arrangements been made?"

"Not yet. After the bodies are released by the coroner, the families will be taking them home for burial. We plan to hold a memorial service here, probably on Thursday, but we haven't sorted out the details. I'll keep you informed."

After I wrote and filed my final story, I went to Moose's office. He was on the phone at his desk, surrounded by stacks of paper. He hung up and motioned me in.

"Can I help you out with those credentials? I've got a bit of time."

"That would be great. I'm just ordering lunch. Want some?"

I accepted, gratefully, and pulled up a chair at the

corner of his desk. He passed a stack of applications to me.

"Put these in piles according to what you know about them. If you've heard of the writer or the paper they're probably okay. Then we'll go over them together."

We worked in companionable silence for half an hour, interrupted only by the constantly ringing phone. Occasionally one of us would read out a name for confirmation or amusement.

"Mary Lynn McConnachy from something called *Sports Today* in Oshawa. Who does she think she's kidding?"

"Get this, Kate. Ryerson journalism school is trying to send a staff of eight. One of them is allegedly doing a thesis on how the media cover a major sporting event."

"Why don't you recommend they try the curling championships in Hamilton next spring?"

"These guys must think the applications are being processed by computers."

"Or extremely naive elves."

When our sandwiches arrived, we took them to the staff lunchroom, but it was full. Moose got us soft drinks from the machine, then set off down the hall.

"I've got to get away from my phone before my head splits. Let's go to the scouts' office. It should be empty."

He found the right key on his ring and let us in to a small, windowless room with a couple of bare desks and a blackboard on the wall. Moose closed the door behind us. The *Sports Illustrated* Swimsuit Calendar was hanging on the back of it. Still turned to June. I could guess why.

"Have you got anything for a headache?"

I dug in my bag and found my pill bottle.

"Two," he said.

"What do you think, Moose? Who done it?"

112

"I don't know. Who could have something against both of them?"

"What if they're not connected? What if someone with a grudge against Thorson took advantage of Sanchez's murder to get rid of Steve?"

"Could be."

"What if Thorson found something out about Sanchez? Then the killer had to shut him up."

"You've been reading too many mysteries, Kate."

"Let's be logical. Gamblers?"

"What's the point of killing Thorson *after* he's pitched?"

"Drugs?"

"Sanchez might have used them, but not Thorson."

"No, he wouldn't tamper with the perfect body. Okay, let's forget motive. What about opportunity?"

"It's got to be someone inside."

"Not necessarily." I told him about the tape on the door between the dugout and the clubhouse.

"What if someone outside had a confederate tape the door so he could get in later. All he'd have to do is hide somewhere in the stadium after the game, then sneak in."

"I wonder what Thorson was doing there?"

"Maybe someone arranged to meet him."

"Funny place for a meeting." Moose crumpled his sandwich wrapper and tossed it towards the wastebasket. It hit the rim and bounced out.

I did the same and made the shot. Swish.

"A buck says you can't do that again."

"Best two out of three," I said, and retrieved the two paper balls.

We each made one of our first two shots. I missed the third, and Moose rebounded his off the bookcase. I dug out my wallet and paid up.

"I do believe I was just hustled. Let's get back to

work. I'll give you another hour. I'm babysitting tonight and I've still got some work to do."

"T.C.?"

"Yeah. He's pretty upset. Sultan was his buddy, especially after he gave him a glove on Saturday."

"That's tough."

He opened the door and held it for me.

We'd sorted through most of the applications by three-thirty. I left him in his office and went to the clubhouse. I asked the constable at the door if Staff Sergeant Munro was free.

He came out looking more rumpled than before. He'd taken off his jacket and rolled up his sleeves. He didn't look happy to see me.

"Something you want to tell me?"

"No. I was just checking in before I leave to see if you had anything to tell me."

"I was going to send for you anyway. Come in here."

We went into the players' lounge, which had become his command post. An extra table had been brought in and was covered with empty coffee cups and ashtrays heaped with butts. A younger man sitting there looked up with interest as we came in.

"Ms Henry, this is Jim Wells, my partner."

He waited for us to exchange greetings, then turned to me, looking grim.

"I don't think you were quite honest with me," he said.

"I don't know what you mean."

"There was an argument between Thorson and Kelsey yesterday afternoon. Why didn't you mention it?"

"I didn't think it was important. That sort of thing goes on all the time. Joe wasn't the only guy he got into arguments with."

"But he is the only one whose bat was used as a murder weapon. Let me decide what's important."

"I didn't know."

"Now you do. Kelsey also has a history of drug abuse and violence that you neglected to mention. Are you sleeping with this guy or something?"

Munro was becoming less attractive the longer I knew him.

"That's a disgusting insinuation," I said. "It doesn't deserve a reply. You've got a warped mind. And that drug story is ancient history. He went through a rehab program three years ago and has tested clean ever since. He's born-again, for heaven's sake. He leads the chapel on Sundays. Surely you can't suspect him?"

"I suspect everyone at this point. We're still checking alibis. I'm sorry if I've insulted you, but I just wish you'd told me about Kelsey and Thorson this morning."

"Who did tell you? Swain? Grabowski?" I could tell by his look that I was close to the mark.

"Those two are flat-out racists. They're good old boys from Texas who talk about niggers and dogs in the same breath. You're taking their word?"

"I'm not taking anyone's word, Ms Henry. I just have to investigate everything I hear."

I guess he was right. I was overreacting. In lieu of an apology, which I couldn't quite choke out, I told him about the reconciliation I'd watched between Thorson and Kelsey after the game. He grunted and made a couple of notes in his book.

"What about Sanchez?" I asked. "Have you found the connection?"

"Not yet. Off the record, do you think Sanchez could have been capable of blackmail?"

I was a bit taken aback.

"I don't know. He wasn't cursed with many scruples. Behind his jovial facade he was driven and a bit paranoid. He saw conspiracies against him because of his colour, his language, his age, you name it. And he was always looking out for himself. I'm not sure what that adds up to. Why do you ask?"

"There are some unexplained large regular entries in his bank account."

"How large?"

"Five figures a month."

"Maybe he'd loaned some money? Maybe pay for endorsements? Bonuses?"

"We're checking it out. Blackmail is just one possibility. I'd rather you didn't print anything about this."

"Not until you tell me I can. I'm glad to help you, as long as I know I'm going to get my story when this is all over."

"I'll give you all you need then."

"That's a deal. If there's nothing else, I've got to run. I'll be at home tonight if you need me."

"Very kind," he said, with an almost straight face.

13

I called Jake Watson before I left the ballpark.

"I'll file from home, Jake. I'm babysitting."

"I need Sandi Thorson," he said.

"Give the lady a break. Her husband's hardly cold."

"We have to get her first, Kate. Get on it."

"I'll try in the morning."

"What are the odds?"

"I wasn't exactly her husband's favourite, Jake."

"No one was. Just use those womanly wiles."

"All right. I'll try. I'll make some calls tonight. I'm sure she won't talk, though."

"It's your neck if she's in the *Mirror* tomorrow."

When I got home, I heard loud music coming from Sally's apartment. I banged on the door on my way upstairs.

"I'm home, T.C. If you're not doing your homework, you're in deep shit!"

Elwy met me at the door, meowing a plaintive tale of imminent starvation. He butted his head against my calves while I opened a can and threaded between my ankles, yapping all the while, as I crossed the kitchen to his dish.

"Bitch, bitch, bitch. That's all you ever do. What about a bit of gratitude for all the work I do to feed you? Hmm?"

He was too busy to answer, trying to eat the food before it finished the trip from the can to his dish.

I phoned down to Sally's.

"Hey, T.C. What have you got down there for supper?"

"Mum's left me macaroni and cheese."

"Great. My personal fave. It will go perfectly with the burgers I'm going to make us. Bring the noodles when you come. I've got to make some calls. I'll see you at six-thirty."

"Okay. That's neat."

"And if you've finished your homework, we'll watch the Yankee game."

"All right!"

I made myself a pot of tea and took it up to my study. My first call was to Gloves Gardiner.

"I need your help," I said. There was no point getting coy with the catcher. "Isn't Karin a good friend of Sandi Thorson?"

"Yeah, she's over there right now."

"I want to interview her. Could Karin put in a word for me? I'd like to get her story as soon as possible."

"Can't you leave her alone for a few days?"

"Unfortunately, she's news and I've got to get to her."

"It isn't like you to be so cold, Kate. I don't want to get involved. Neither does Karin."

"Just ask. Tell her if Sandi doesn't talk to somebody she's going to have every reporter in the city camped outside her door. If she talks to one person, it will get the rest off her back. And wouldn't she rather talk to me than to one of those sleazoids from the *Mirror*? I'm

118

not going to do a hatchet job on her, for God's sake. She's a widow. Trust me."

"I don't know. I'll ask Karin what she thinks when she gets home. I can't promise anything."

"There's something else. About the murder motive."

He laughed. "I can think of about twenty. Can't you?"

I crossed my fingers for the promise I was about to bend a little.

"I can't tell you why, but I think maybe Sanchez was blackmailing someone."

"It wasn't me."

"Think about it. Did anyone seem really relieved when they heard he was dead?"

"No. We were all shocked."

"What about the reaction to Thorson?"

"Now we're scared."

"How so?"

"Sultan could have been killed by anyone in Toronto. Steve's murderer has to be someone we know. We're watching our backs."

"Oh, Gloves, no."

"'Fraid so. I gotta go. See you tomorrow."

"Get Karin to call me." I gave him my number.

My next call was to Tiny Washington. We covered most of the same ground. He said he wasn't being blackmailed either.

"Tiny, did you know it was Preacher's bat that killed Thorson?"

Munro hadn't said I couldn't tell anyone, just that I shouldn't print it.

"Do they think he did it?"

"They also know about the fight on Sunday."

"Who told them?"

"It wasn't me. Was it you?"

"Stinger and Grabowski."

"That's my guess."

"They think Preacher's stupid enough to kill some-one with his own bat?"

"Who knows. If you're talking to any of the guys, ask if they know anything about any blackmail, okay?"

"What are you doing, playing detective?"

"Just chasing a story, Tiny. Keep in touch."

"Yes, ma'am." Tiny sounded amused.

I finished the story I had started at the ballpark. I didn't have much more than gossip and off-the-record stuff, but I managed to pull something together.

When I was done, I changed into a leotard and tights and spent half an hour at the barre. The workout was long overdue. My knees creaked in the pliés. My hamstrings screamed on the tendus. I'd been playing hooky from class for the last six weeks. Madame would not be pleased.

T.C. was at the door promptly at six-thirty. He was juggling a casserole, a schoolbook, and Sultan's glove, his prized possession – he probably slept with it. His glasses had slipped down his nose. I relieved him of the casserole before it fell.

"I didn't quite finish my homework," he said. "I've got another chapter to read."

"Perfect," I said. "I've got to take a shower anyway. Why don't you get yourself a Pepsi out of the fridge – I won't tell your mum – and read your chapter. Then we can talk."

I turned the bathroom radio to *As It Happens* while I let the shower wash away the day. I bumped it up to the hottest it would deliver and let the spray massage some of the tension kinks out of my back. I felt almost human when I was done.

I was crashing about in the kitchen, doing my world-famous imitation of a domestic person, when T.C. came in.

"Can I help? My homework's done."

"Just sit yourself down and tell me your news."

"Have they found anything out about the murders yet?"

"I don't think so."

"Why would someone want to kill them?"

"I don't know, honey."

"It's not fair."

I didn't want to tell him that life's not fair. He was already finding that out sooner than most kids.

"Don't worry, they'll catch whoever did it. The detective in charge of the investigation seems like a pretty sharp guy."

"Yeah? What's he like? Like on *Miami Vice*?"

Enough of this morbid curiosity.

"So, listen. Did your friends like your new glove?"

"They thought it was pretty neat," he said. "Do you realize that I'm probably the last kid he ever gave anything to?"

Good changing of subject, Kate.

"Do you want cheese on your burger?"

"Okay. Kate, do you know anything about gloves?"

"Try me."

"The stitching's coming loose. Can you fix it?"

"Probably. I've watched other people do it. I'll look at it after dinner. Do you want to watch TV while we eat?"

"Yeah. Great!"

I put together a tray with cutlery and condiments and sent him up to my study with it. When I followed ten minutes later with the food, a glass of milk for him, and a beer for me, he was engrossed in *The Dating Game*.

"Who do you think he should choose, kid?"

"Bachelorette number three."

"How come?"

"She's got the biggest tits."

T.C. was growing up. I pretended to be shocked and he blushed.

We had a nice evening curled up on the couch. The Yankees were beating the Red Sox so badly by nine-fifteen that T.C. didn't even complain when I sent him down to get ready for bed. I turned off the set and carried the dishes to the kitchen.

A moment later, he was back.

"There's something wrong downstairs, Kate."

"What do you mean?"

"The back door's open."

"You must have forgotten to close it."

"No. It was locked before. I know it was."

"I'll go check. You wait here."

"Don't go down there. What if someone's hiding?"

The kid had a point. I dialled 911. The operator answered on the third ring. I gave her my address and told her the problem. A police cruiser pulled up no more than seven minutes later. Pretty good.

T.C. and I went through the apartment with the officers, once they had established that there were no criminals lurking in the closets. Nothing seemed to be missing.

"It could be that he ran away when you came in, son. Was the front door locked?"

I was a bit embarrassed.

"No. I don't usually lock it until I go to bed."

"What about the apartment doors?"

"I didn't lock it," T.C. said. "I was just coming upstairs. I didn't think I had to. My mum's going to be mad."

"Don't worry about that." I put my arm around him.

"When will she be home? Does she leave the boy alone often?"

"He's not alone. He's with me. T.C., get your pajamas and toothbrush. You can sleep in my bed until she gets home."

The police took another fifteen minutes to take down our story. They didn't seem terribly concerned. I guess they thought that anyone stupid enough to leave doors unlocked deserved what they got. They were probably right. When they left, I locked up and left a note for Sally on her door.

Upstairs, I tucked T.C. in and unplugged the bedroom phone.

"Sleep tight, honey. Your mother will be home pretty soon."

14

I'd just turned out the bedroom light when Karin Gardiner phoned.

"Sandi Thorson will give you an interview tomorrow," she said. "Can you be at her house at ten?"

"Of course. Thank you, Karin. How is she?"

"She's fine. I'm not sure it's really sunk in yet."

"Do you know what her plans are?"

"No. Her parents have been here for a few days. So that's a help. And Steve's parents got here this morning."

"And that's no help at all, right?"

"You could say that."

I had heard stories about Thorson's parents, a rather unpleasant couple who had neglected him as a child, then rushed to cash in once he made it.

"I'll try not to make it any more difficult for her."

"Thank you. Sandi asked me to be there during the interview, if you don't mind."

She gave me the address and we said good-bye. I went up to the study and pulled my file on Thorson. Shortly after eleven I heard Sally at the door.

"What's happened? Where's T.C.?"

"He's fine. He's sleeping in my bed. Don't worry about him. Let me get us a drink."

Sally was already a bit drunk from her gallery opening, but I figured one more wouldn't hurt her. I certainly wanted one. I mixed a couple of Scotch and waters and explained what had happened.

"I'll go downstairs with you, if you like, to check things out, but I don't think anything is missing."

"In a minute. You didn't hear anything?"

"I'm sorry, Sally. We were on the third floor."

"I should never have left him alone. What if something had happened?"

"You didn't leave him alone, Sally. You left him with me. And he's fine."

"Kidnappers. What if it was kidnappers?"

"After your vast wealth, no doubt. I don't think so."

"His father. It was Roger trying to steal him from me."

"Sally, Roger sees him whenever he wants. Why would he want to steal him? He doesn't want a full-time child. You know that."

"I guess you're right. Can we go down now?"

"Sure, no problem."

We started down the stairs, Sally in the lead.

I started to ask her about her party and she turned, finger to her lips, and shushed me, her eyes big. She was tiptoeing.

"I think they've left," I whispered. "You're just going to scare yourself."

At the door, she hesitated.

"For heaven's sake, give me the key," I said, in a normal voice, and opened the door. I had left the lights on. Sally held back until I was in the kitchen.

"Coast is clear, Sal. Come look."

She came in, laughing nervously.

"I'm being a wimp."

I agreed.

We made a tour of the apartment. Nothing was missing.

"It was probably just kids. You're lucky you haven't got anything worth stealing."

"Wait a minute. What do you mean? What about the television set? My jewellery? My . . ."

"There's not much of a market for fourteen-inch black-and-white TV sets, Sally. Your jewellery, while charming, would not set a fence's soul aquiver. Now, your collection of pigs. I'm amazed they missed those."

"What about my fabulous wardrobe and priceless art?"

We both giggled.

"Hey, why don't you bring some things up and spend the night. You can bunk in with T.C. I'll sleep in my study. It won't seem so bad in the morning."

"All right. Do we have to go to sleep right now?"

"No. We'll have another drink, and talk."

"Oh, good. A slumber party. I've got to tell you about the guy I met tonight."

"Right." I steered her out the door.

Sally was full of news about the opening – a retrospective of a brilliant, eccentric photographer. The Mayor had been there, and the Minister of Culture. Mercifully, both had left before the photographer called the art critic from the *Mirror* a slut and she threw a drink in his face.

"Thank God no one with money reads the *Mirror*," she giggled. "So, we had to go out to dinner afterwards and have a few bottles of wine to recover. How's your day been?"

I ran through it for her. Towards the end of the story I remembered my promise to T.C.

"I'd better see what I can do with that glove. It's in the kitchen. Fix us another drink while I get it."

I could see what T.C. meant. The leather lacing was

loose at the base of the thumb, pulled out from the palm piece.

"This is more complicated than I thought. I'm going to have to undo the whole thing and put it back together."

"Are you sure? T.C.'s not going to be happy if he finds his glove in pieces all over the floor."

"Well, if I screw it up too badly, I can take it to the ballpark tomorrow and get someone to fix it. Besides, it's a challenge. The amazing Kate Henry never shirks a challenge."

"Hear, hear!" Sally raised her glass.

I started at the top of the thumb, where the lacing was knotted. It wasn't too hard to pull it out, using a nail file. I was halfway across the palm piece when the padding began to come out.

"Oh, shit, Sally, look at this."

"What?"

Only the very edge of the padding was the grey felt I expected to find. Behind it were plastic bags full of white powder. I had not lived a totally sheltered life.

"If this is what I think, I know what the murderer was looking for in Sanchez's apartment. And maybe in yours, Sally."

"Oh, my God."

"I'm calling the cops."

There was no home number on the card Staff Sergeant Munro had given me, and the duty officer at the office told me he couldn't be reached.

"I know it's late, but could you have him call me? It's Kate Henry calling about the Sanchez case. I've discovered something that I think he'll want to know about."

"He really doesn't want to be disturbed tonight, Miss Henry. Maybe I could help you."

"No offence, but I'd rather talk to the staff sergeant. And it can't wait until tomorrow."

"I'll call him right away. I just want to warn you that if it's not important, he's going to be mad."

"Oh, I'm sure she'll understand, Officer."

I could hear him stifling a laugh as he hung up.

It was obviously time to switch to coffee. I made a pot and brought a couple of cups into the living room.

"You don't have to wait up."

"You think I could sleep?"

Five minutes later, a grumpy sounding Staff Sergeant Munro was on the phone.

"What is it, Ms Henry?"

"I hope I didn't wake you up, Staff Sergeant."

"You didn't."

"I think I know why Sultan Sanchez was murdered."

"Yeah?" He didn't sound thrilled.

"What about drugs?"

"Ms Henry, I didn't call you at quarter to one in the morning to play guessing games. What have you got?"

"I've got a glove, Staff Sergeant. A baseball glove that Sultan Sanchez gave to a young friend of mine. A baseball glove packed with what appears to be cocaine. I'm sorry if you think that's a game."

"I'll be right there."

He took my address and hung up.

"He's on his way. I'm going to change."

"Why?"

"You'll know when you see him," I said.

I crept into my bedroom and took a pair of linen slacks and a silk blouse out of the closet without waking T.C. — casual but elegant. I put on enough makeup to look good, but not enough to notice. Then I opened a new pack of cigarettes.

I heard a car door shut and went to the window. Munro was locking a Volkswagen Beetle a few doors down the street. Not your average cop. I went down-stairs to let him in.

"Thanks for coming," I said, leading him up the stairs. I introduced him to Sally and didn't miss her appreciative look. He was wearing a pair of baggy sweat pants and a cotton sweater. So much for dressing up.

"It was her son Sultan gave the glove to," I explained. "They live downstairs."

I offered Munro a coffee.

"Black, with three sugars, please."

I must have made a face.

"It's one of my few vices."

I showed him the glove and explained how T.C. had got it, how I had come to take it apart, and about the break-in.

"Who knew the boy had the glove?"

"Tiny Washington was there when he got it. Any number of people on the field could have seen him with it."

"He was talking to some of the players on Sunday, too, Kate. I think he even got some autographs on the glove."

Of course. I picked it up.

"Joe Kelsey, Stinger Swain, Alex Jones, Slider Holmes, Gloves Gardiner, Mark Griffin. A lot of the players knew T.C., Staff Sergeant. He's been down on the field with me a couple of times. He's a nice kid."

"I'm sure he is. I'll have to talk to him."

"Now?"

"No. Let him sleep. I'll get together with him tomorrow."

"Should I keep him home from school?"

"It might be a good idea. Whoever wants that glove doesn't know we've got it. I assume the boy has been taking it with him wherever he goes, right?"

"You know kids."

"I've got a couple myself," he smiled. Married.

"I see them as often as I can," he continued. Divorced. I was glad I'd gone with casual but elegant. "My son's a big ball fan. He'll be jealous when he hears I've met you, Ms Henry."

"Call me Kate, for heaven's sake."

"All right. I'm Andy."

"But your name's Lloyd."

"It's an old family name. I'm the fourth generation. My middle name's Andrew and my friends are kind enough to use it."

"Well, I guess I'll get to bed," Sally said, subtle as a crutch. "Nice to have met you, Staff Sergeant."

"Someone will be in touch with you in the morning."

"If I'm not at home, I'll be at the gallery. I'll take T.C. with me. Kate can give you the phone numbers."

After she left, we sat for a few moments in awkward silence.

"More coffee? Or could I offer you a drink? Unless you can't drink on duty."

"Well, I'm off duty, technically. I'd love a Scotch, if you've got some."

"With water?"

"Just a bit. And one ice cube."

"No sugar?"

"Not in Scotch, thanks."

When we had settled in with our drinks, we both started to talk at once.

"You first," I laughed.

"I've been thinking about you," he said.

"Oh?"

"There are a couple of things I'd like to talk to you about, but I don't want it all over the papers."

"I won't print any of it until an arrest is made, as long as I get an exclusive."

"You've got a deal. Do you have a cassette recorder?"

131

"Yes, in my study. Why?"

"I've got a tape for you to listen to. See if you recognize any of the voices."

"Where does it come from?"

"Sultan Sanchez's answering machine. It's the messages that were recorded on Saturday night."

I got my portable recorder. The sound quality wasn't great, but I had no problem with the first caller.

"Hi, honey, it's Ginny. It's seven o'clock. I'm at the Fillet. Where are you? If you're listening in, get your sweet buns down here. Bye bye." Kissing noises followed.

"Sultan had a number of friends in town when his wife wasn't here," I said. "I ran into that one on Saturday, as a matter of fact. She was pretty drunk by midnight."

"Yes, I could tell. She called back several times."

The second call was a man's voice.

"I've got the money. I'll be at Brandy's at eleven."

"He called again, too. Is the voice familiar?"

"I'm not sure."

He rewound it and played it again.

"I'll have to think about it."

The next call was in Spanish, a woman speaking.

"This is from another, um, friend of his," Munro said. "She's telling him she wants his body, approximately."

"Popular fella. Do you speak Spanish?"

"No. One of the translators at headquarters listened to it for me."

"I would imagine Alex Jones might be able to tell you who she is."

The fourth call was a crank call, some drunken fan telling him he was a bum for striking out.

"How do they get these guys' unlisted phone numbers? I had to work my butt off to get them."

The fifth was from Ginny again.

"Hi, honey," she said, sounding a bit frail. "I'm still at the Fillet. We're holding the champagne and cake until you get here, so hurry."

There was a lot of background noise on the next call.

"I've been at Brandy's for half an hour. I'm tired of waiting. I'll get to you after the game tomorrow."

"I still can't recognize it. It's hard with all the noise."

"Just one more."

"You bastard," Ginny's voice slurred. "You don't stand me up and get away with it. We're through." The phone was slammed down.

"That's it. I was hoping you'd recognize the man's voice."

"Was it a drug deal, do you think? That would explain the large sums of money going into his bank account."

"Perhaps. We'll know better tomorrow. We found a safety deposit key in his valuables drawer at the ballpark. We'll see what he's got in it."

"Why don't you ask at Brandy's and find out if any ballplayers were in there on Saturday."

"We did actually think of that all by ourselves, Kate." He fought the smile. "That's assuming it's a ballplayer. There was a full house at Brandy's that night, including no less than five Titans and seven Red Sox."

"Right. Who were the Titans?"

"Stinger Swain, Moe Grabowski, Eddie Carter, Joe Kelsey, and Slider Holmes."

"Not all together, I assume."

"Nope. Like you said. The whites were in one group and the blacks in another."

"Did anyone notice who was in there for just half an hour?"

"With that mob, we're lucky anyone noticed anything."

"I'm trying to figure which of them might be into drugs."

"I think you might be barking up the wrong investigative tree, Kate."

"You mean drugs? What's that right there on the table?"

"Drugs. And where did the drugs come from?"

"Sultan Sanchez's glove."

"Which he gave away to an eleven-year-old boy. Which suggests what?"

"That he didn't know the glove was full of drugs."

"Bingo. Your average drug dealer seldom gives away close to a pound of cocaine."

"You've made your point."

"Thank you." He stood up. "I think I'll leave while I'm ahead. Past my bedtime."

"I'm sorry. I didn't realize. Do you want a bag for the glove and stuff?"

"No. I'll take it like this. Tell the boy I'll get the glove back to him as soon as I can. And call me if you remember that voice."

I stuck out my hand. He shook it solemnly.

"Thanks for the coffee. And the drink. And the suggestions." At the door he turned. "And don't forget to lock the door. Good night."

While I made up the couch in the study, a surprisingly small part of my mind was engaged in thinking how good the Staff Sergeant looked in sweats. Most of it was worrying and wondering.

Specifically, worrying about Joe Kelsey and wondering whether I should have told Andy that it was Joe's voice on the tape.

15

Sally woke me with a cup of tea in hand.

"It's almost nine," she said. "Don't you have to be somewhere at ten?"

"Thanks. How's T.C.? Did you tell him about the glove?"

"I didn't know how much I should tell him. I just said the police needed it for evidence and he'd get it back when they were through. He's so excited about skipping school that he hasn't asked any questions."

"Good. I'm going to have to rush."

I gulped the first cup of tea in the shower. Sally brought me a piece of toast and marmalade while I dressed and T.C. nattered at me while I put on makeup. I was out of there in twenty-five minutes with a half-hour drive ahead of me, if there wasn't too much traffic.

The Thorsons lived in the same waterfront condominium complex as half a dozen other players, a modern tower poking out of several acres of parkland. The concierge stopped just short of asking me for my mother's maiden name before he let me in.

I could hear a child crying as I knocked nervously on the penthouse door. Karin Gardiner let me in. Sandi Thorson was on her knees, comforting her sturdy little two-year-old, kissing away his hurt.

"Stevie fell," Karin explained.

I made sympathetic noises and looked around. The view of the lake was spectacular, but otherwise it looked like any other dull modern apartment.

"Come on, Pooch," Sandi said. "I'll get you some juice and you can watch *Sesame Street*. You want to see Big Bird?"

The kid's face lit up, and he ran down the hall, shrieking "Sesame, Sesame!" in delight.

His mother filled a bottle with apple juice and handed it to Karin, who took it to the boy. She cut short my apologies for disturbing her.

"Do you mind if we talk in the kitchen?"

"That's fine."

Looking into the living room, I could see why. It was filled with trophies and framed newspaper clippings, a shrine to her husband. The kitchen was her turf, filled with cheerful domesticity. There were letter magnets on the fridge at Stevie level and cartoons and lists at grownup height. We sat on padded stools at a counter in the corner that had a fresh pot of coffee at one end. Sandi poured into three flowered mugs.

"How's Stevie doing?"

"I don't think he really knows what's happened. He thinks his father's just on another road trip. I'm doing my best to keep things as normal as I can."

"That can't be easy."

She looked at me as if I were crazy.

Karin came into the kitchen and sat down.

"Stevie's fine." Sandi nodded, and the three of us sat for a moment in awkward silence.

"I'll try to make this as painless as possible. Can you tell me about Sunday night?"

She used both hands to push her streaked blonde hair off her face. It wasn't clean and looked as if it hadn't been brushed. She was dressed in jeans and a man's rugger shirt, striped in green and blue. She was washed out without makeup, and her eyes were puffy. The diamonds in her ears and on a gold chain around her neck looked harshly frivolous against her skin.

"We got home about six and had dinner with my folks. After we heard about Sultan we didn't feel much like celebrating. Just after we finished, Steve got a phone call from Tony Marsden, a friend of ours. He runs the car dealership we lease from.

"He invited Steve to go fishing on the off day. He said it was probably the last chance of the year and the weather was going to be good. Steve had been to his cottage before. He really wanted to go, but there was a players' meeting. So he called Ted Ferguson to ask permission and told him he wanted to play the rest of the season.

"Ted said he could go, so Steve left at about seven-thirty. He had left his gear at the stadium after his last trip, so he was going to pick it up and drive from there up to the cottage to get an early start.

"And that's the last time I saw him. Alive."

She stopped and stared into her coffee cup.

"We had a fight before he left. His folks were arriving in the morning and he expected me to take care of them all day while he was fishing. I don't get along with them very well. They didn't approve of our marriage. I was divorced when I met him, and he was a big star. They think I'm after his money.

"It was one of those whisper fights, you know? I didn't want my mom and dad to hear us. I try to hide any problems when they're around."

She paused again, and her eyes filled with tears.

"The last thing I said to him was that if he went to Tony's cottage he shouldn't bother to come home. But I didn't mean it."

She began to cry in earnest.

"I lay in bed that night thinking up ways to get even. And he was probably dead by then."

Karin put her arms around her sobbing friend and glared at me. I tried to look blameless.

"I'm sorry," Sandi said, fumbling at a box of tissues. She blew her nose, then pushed the hair off her face again.

"I just can't help spilling my guts out these days."

"I understand. I'm sorry I have to make you go through it again."

"It's not your fault. Let's go on."

"Is there anything you can think of that could explain what happened?"

"I've been trying to figure that out, and I just can't. I know that Steve didn't have a lot of friends, but he didn't have real enemies either, not ones that would want to kill him. He could be difficult, sometimes, but he wasn't harmful. All I keep coming up with is Sam Craven. Did he hate Steve enough to kill him? I don't know. I like Sam, but he was real angry at Steve. He was in Toronto that day, too."

"What about a motive? Surely Sam would profit most by changing Steve's mind."

"Steve wasn't going to change his mind. No way."

"What about links between him and Sanchez? Were they connected off the field in any way?"

Something evasive passed across her eyes, then was gone. She looked firmly at me and shook her head.

"The problem with it being Sam Craven is, how could he have known Steve was going to the stadium? Unless they had arranged to meet there."

"Steve would never have arranged to meet him without telling me. But what about if Sam was following him?"

She had a point.

"I don't know how to put this, but could there be some personal reason someone might be out to get him?"

"You mean an irate husband or something? I thought of that, of course. But I don't think so. Look, I'm not stupid. None of us are as dumb as our husbands think. I've known about Steve's women on the road since one of them answered the phone when I called him to tell him I was going into the hospital to have Stevie. But he never cheated on me here. He wouldn't dare."

I believed her. I had underestimated Sandi. Because of her looks and dress, or perhaps the way she spelled her name. She was no bimbo.

We talked for half an hour more about Thorson and their life together, about her anger and fear, and the loneliness she was just starting to feel. We talked about her plans, too. She hoped to go back to school one day for a master's degree and get a job, options that had been denied her as a baseball wife. But not until the child she was carrying was in school. It would be hard enough for the kids to cope without having a father.

"What happens now?"

"After the funeral I guess I'll go back to Denver with my parents and wait for the baby."

"There's one more thing. When I told you all that Sultan Sanchez was dead, you fainted. Why?"

The evasive look came back.

"It was hot in the lounge," Karin said, quickly. "Sandi's been having a bit of trouble with the pregnancy."

"Was that it?"

"Yes. That was it."

Something was going on.

"Look. I think maybe I know. I'm not going to write

about it — not yet, anyway, and never with any details — but I'd like you to tell me if I'm on the right track. Was Sanchez blackmailing Steve?"

Their faces told me I was right.

"How did you know?"

"I can't tell you that. Have you told the police?"

"No, of course not."

"Do you know where Steve was on Saturday night?"

"He was with me. He didn't kill Sanchez. I swear it."

"How long had the blackmail been going on?"

"All season. Sultan found out something . . . about Steve's past. At spring training, he told him that he would tell the story unless Steve paid him money. We paid him $5,000 every month."

"Forgive me, but that doesn't seem like a lot of money for someone making Steve's salary."

"I don't think it was just the money. I think Sanchez liked having control over us. He was a terrible man."

"What did he have on Steve? Was it so bad?"

"I can't tell you."

"I understand. But this could be tied up with the murders. Do you know anyone else he was blackmailing?"

"No."

She got up and began to rinse out the coffee cups. I took my cue.

"If you think of anything else, please let me know. I appreciate you giving me this time, Sandi. I really hope things work out for you."

"Thank you for being understanding."

Karin Gardiner walked with me to the elevator.

"You'll be careful, won't you? She shouldn't have told you. She doesn't realize how it might look."

"But it might help catch a murderer. Don't worry. I'm not going to write anything about blackmail."

As the elevator came, we shook hands.

"Trust me," I said.

"I haven't much choice."

15

I went from Sandi's to the office. I tried to reach Joe Kelsey, but he wasn't at home or with Eddie Carter. I left a message for him with Carter's wife, then called the gallery. Sally answered.

"How's T.C.?"

"Great. He thinks it's all a terrific adventure."

"I'm worried about you both."

"Don't worry. Your cute cop friend has sent an inconspicuous young man to stay with us for the next couple of days. I've put him to work helping T.C. with his homework. I called the school and got some assignments. There was one creepy thing, though."

"What's that?"

"The principal's office said that a man had called, someone saying he was his father. He said he was going to pick him up after school. Roger is still in Windsor, and he didn't call."

"Someone's looking for him, or the glove. The break-in wasn't a coincidence."

"Exactly."

"I don't like it."

"I'm not too fond of it myself, but we're well protected."

"Good. I'll call you from the ballpark and see you when I get home."

"Okay. Don't worry."

I was working on my story when Jake Watson wandered by.

"What have you got?"

"Bereaved widow ponders the meaning of life and death, while small son with big blue eyes wonders where his daddy's gone. And she's not pondering it anywhere else but the *Planet*."

"That's my girl."

"Right. Am I covering alone tonight?"

"No. Glebe's going to be there to do a column. Do you need any more help?"

"At some point I will. You're working me pretty hard these days."

"I'll make it up to you when the season's over."

"If I last that long."

"You can do it, kid."

"Not if you don't leave me alone and let me finish this heart-rending piece of work."

"I'll buy you a beer when you're done."

"You're on."

I'd finished by three-thirty and Jake and I adjourned to the Final Edition, the bar on the main floor of the Planet building. It was full of the drunken dregs of the lunch crowd, complaining about their editors' insensitivity, churlishness, and general stupidity. The same scene was played out by the same crowd almost every day. We managed to get the waitress's attention and ordered a couple of beers, cold and fast.

"That was a tough one. I like Sandi Thorson. She's going through a hard time."

"I'm surprised at your sentimentality, Kate."

"This cactus-like exterior hides a sensitive flower underneath, boss. You know that."

"Yeah, sure. What else have you got? Any line on the killer?"

"None I can write about yet, but there's some interesting stuff I can use after it's over."

I told him what Munro had told me and what I'd been able to dig up about blackmail. I also told him that I had recognized Kelsey's voice on the tape from Sanchez's apartment. Jake was a friend as well as a boss, and I trusted him absolutely. He wouldn't betray a confidence, and I needed him as a sounding board.

"The problem is, none of it hangs together. Thorson appears to have had a motive, but if he killed Sanchez, who killed Thorson? And it certainly couldn't have been Thorson in Sally's apartment last night."

"Have you talked to Munro today?"

"Not yet. I want to talk to Joe Kelsey first."

"Are you sure? You're taking a risk."

"Not at the ballpark. There are lots of people around. Besides, I know it couldn't be Joe."

"Just be careful."

I finished my beer, stood up, and saluted.

"Yessir, boss. I'll talk to you later."

I went back to the office and picked up a phone message from Andy Munro. No more "Staff Sergeant Munro," eh? I put it in my pocket and left for the ballpark.

I went immediately to the Titan clubhouse, which the police had reopened. No Joe. I went into the players' lounge, which was empty. I heard noises from the weight room and poked my head around the corner. Joe was there, alone, working on one of the machines.

"Hi, Kate," he grunted. "I got your message. Sorry I didn't call back."

"That's okay. I knew where to find you. Can we talk?"

"For a minute."

I didn't know how to begin.

"This is a bit tough, Preacher. We've got to talk, but you must trust me. What you tell me never has to come out."

He stopped working the machine and picked up a towel.

"Yeah?"

"I heard a tape of the messages left on Sultan's answering machine Saturday night. The police wanted to see if I recognized any of the voices. I lied and told them I didn't."

He wiped his face and sat down on a bench.

"They're going to ask you about it eventually. They know which players were at Brandy's that night."

"What if I did call?"

"Preacher, was Sultan blackmailing you?"

"Why are you asking?"

"I know he was blackmailing at least one other player. Was that why you were calling him? You said something about having the money. If it wasn't blackmail, the police think it was for drugs. Which was it?"

"Not drugs, Kate. I'm through with that. I swear it."

I wanted to believe him.

"You've got to talk, Joe. They're suspicious of you because of the bat and because of your fight with Steve. This is no time to be hiding anything."

I put my hand on his arm.

"Kate, believe me. There are some things I have to hide."

"And Sultan found out?"

He nodded, and was about to speak when Stinger Swain walked in. He stopped, then leered at us.

I stepped back, embarrassed.

"Looking for some Christian counselling, Miss Lonelyhearts? Or is God's own Superstar looking for a bit of ink? Or are you both looking for a little privacy?"

"Shut up, Stinger." Kelsey brushed past him and left the room.

"Do you work at being an asshole, Swain?"

"Watch your language, Katie, baby. You wouldn't want me to think you're not a lady, now, would you?"

He was still laughing, a horrible cackling sound, when I went out the door.

I looked for Joe, but he was shagging fly balls in right field. He avoided me until it was time for the press to leave the field.

Gloves Gardiner had nothing new to tell me.

"Look, Gloves. I know that Sanchez was blackmailing at least two players. That could be why he was killed, but I'd bet big money it was neither of the two I know about. Are you sure you can't think of anything a little bit out of the ordinary that might help?"

"There's one thing. Karin and I were out for dinner a couple of weeks ago and we ran into Sultan having a drink with David Sloane. Sultan was drinking, that is, not Sloane."

"That's an odd couple."

"Yeah, especially in Toronto. David usually spends all his time at home with his family."

"Thanks. I'll check it out."

"Just split the reward with me when you've captured the killer." He grinned.

"Will do."

Sloane was at the bat rack.

"I need to talk to you," I began.

"Not now. I've got batting practice."

"It's important. Just a few minutes."

"Make it fast."

If that's the way he wanted it, I wouldn't waste time.

147

"Why was Sultan Sanchez blackmailing you?"

"What are you talking about?"

"Sanchez was blackmailing you. I think it may have something to do with his murder."

"And I think you're nuts."

"You don't know what I'm talking about?"

"Sorry to disappoint you."

He chose a bat and trotted to the batting cage. He was staring at me a few moments later, but he looked away quickly when I caught his eye. I couldn't read his expression.

The law finally caught up with me in the press dining room. Andy Munro moved some dirty plates to the next table and sat down across from me.

"You're not very good at returning phone calls."

"I was busy. Besides, I thought you'd be here."

"And here I am."

"What's up? You called me."

"I was just checking to see if you were all right."

"I didn't know the police were so concerned about their witnesses."

"The police aren't. I am."

"Oh."

"We've found out who made that call, by the way. It was Joe Kelsey. I'm surprised you didn't recognize his voice. Isn't he a friend of yours?"

"Well, I guess all the background noise . . ."

"Come off it."

"I wasn't sure."

"I can appreciate that you want to protect your friends, but did it ever occur to you that you might just protect the wrong one? And you might discover your mistake too late for your own good."

"I'm not protecting anyone."

"Besides, I don't appreciate your mistrust."

"But —"

"We're not in the business of fabricating evidence and harassing innocent people, no matter what you think."

"I didn't —"

"You didn't what? Didn't lie to me? I've talked to Kelsey. He told me about your conversation. Who are you, Nancy Drew? Leave it to the professionals. It's a dangerous business, and I don't need amateurs messing up my investigation. So butt out."

I tried to defend myself.

"I'm in the investigation business, too, you know. I'm a reporter trying to get a story, that's all."

"Just don't keep things from me any more."

Moose's arrival saved me from making promises.

"You've got a call in the press box, Kate."

It was Sally.

"Bad news, Kate. Last night's prowler came back sometime today. He went through your place, too. It's a mess. The police are here now."

"Oh, no. Is anything gone?"

"I don't think so. He just dumped all the drawers and went through everything."

"Damn. Is Elwy all right?"

"Yes. But it looks like your friend Andy was guarding the wrong thing. He should have put one of his people here instead of with me and T.C."

"Exactly. I just might mention it to him, too."

Munro was in the corridor. I didn't waste any time.

"Where were we? Oh, right. You were telling me to leave things to the professionals? Does one of your professionals want to put my house back together? While your professionals were busy doing whatever it is professionals do, my house was being trashed."

"Damn."

"So don't give me any more crap about not getting involved. I'm involved."

Not a bad exit line. I turned and marched back into the press box, only ruining the effect slightly by tripping on a wastebasket on the way to my seat.

"What was that all about?" asked Moose.

"Stupid cop tries to tell me how to do my job when he can't even do his own."

"What happened?"

I told him about the break-in.

"And that insufferable jerk tells me to keep out of his precious investigation."

"He may be a jerk, but he's probably right, Kate. You could get into trouble. It could be dangerous."

"So could driving to work, Moose. That doesn't mean I'm going to stop doing it."

"I just don't want to see you in any danger."

"I'm a big girl. I'm not going to get into anything I can't handle."

There was a minute of silence before the game began. The Titan starters stood at their positions with their heads bowed, caps held over their hearts, facing the flags in centre field. Each wore a double black armband on his left sleeve. The other Titans and the Tigers lined up in front of the dugouts in the same pose.

It was eerie. The stadium was filled to the rafters, as usual for a series against the Tigers. There were dozens of buses from Detroit in the parking lot, and almost as many fans wore Tiger colours as wore those of the Titans. But they were all so quiet, even after the game began.

"Spooky, isn't it?" Jeff Glebe sat down next to me.

"It sure doesn't feel like a ballgame."

By the seventh inning, the game seemed to have gone on forever. Flakey Patterson was behind most of the hitters, and he littered the basepaths with runners in every inning. Helped by good fielding and luck, he held the Tigers to two runs, but the Titans couldn't score. The fans didn't seem to mind. They stayed quiet.

These games didn't matter, except to the Tigers, who wanted second-place money.

Red was resting a lot of the starters, but he didn't want the team to go into a losing streak to end the season. They had to keep sharp to get into the World Series.

The crowd stirred when David Sloane led off the sixth with a double. Billy Saunders, the Tiger manager, walked to the mound signalling for his righthanded reliever, with three righthanded hitters due up.

I took advantage of the pause in the action to go get a cup of tea. Moose handed me a slip of paper when I got back to my seat. I looked at it, then stuck it in my pocket while Moose watched, none too subtly. Andy Munro could wait.

Gloves walked. Billy Wise was due up, but he was called back to the dugout. Orca Elliott took his place.

"Why doesn't he leave Wise in to bunt?" Jeff Glebe was second-guessing immediately.

"Red doesn't believe in bunting. It's against his religion," I said. "Orca only leads the team in double plays."

As I spoke, Elliott rolled an easy grounder to the Tiger second baseman, who bobbled it, trying to throw to second before he had it in his hand, and the bases were suddenly loaded.

"Horseshoes up his ass," I said.

The fans, glad for an excuse, began to cheer and clap their gloved hands, making a strangely muffled din. There were a couple of pitchers up in the bullpen, a righthander and a lefthander, but Eddie Carter, due up, was a switch hitter. Saunders stayed put.

He probably regretted it when Carter took the fastball they tried to sneak by him and lined it into the power alley in right centre field. While two outfielders chased it all three runners scored and Carter ended up on third. He scored on Alex Jones's sacrifice fly to the warning track in right. With two out, Kid Cooper, playing in Washington's place, hit a home run to give Patterson a three-run cushion.

Flakey used every bit of it. It took a bases-loaded double play in the ninth to end the game. Final score, 5–4 Titans.

With all the late action, it took me longer than usual to file my first story and get down to the clubhouse. When David Sloane saw me coming, he raised his hand, palm out, in a dismissive gesture.

"Not in the clubhouse," he said.

"Lighten up, Sloane. I'm just trying to do my job."

"Do it somewhere else."

He took his street clothes out of his locker on hangers and, in full uniform, marched to the trainer's room to change. Moron.

"You didn't miss much," said Toby King. "He thanked the Lord for giving him the opportunity to help the team."

I made a few retching sounds and went to see Eddie Carter, who was talking with Kid Cooper and Tiny Washington.

"Mr. Speed and Mr. Power, how are you both tonight? You better watch out, Tiny. The Kid's after your job."

"He can have it, soon enough. I hear you're playing detective these days."

"No. I just don't know how to keep my nose out of a good story."

"You be careful, hear?"

"Can you gents give me a couple of quotes about the game?"

"Like I said all along, when the leaves turn brown, we'll be wearing the crown," Eddie said, posing regally, a towel wrapped around his shoulders.

"But you better remember who's the king around here, Carter."

"Yes, your highness," Carter said, bowing in Washington's direction.

Joe Kelsey sat at his locker, on the other side of Carter, quietly ignoring the foolery.

"Hey, Preacher. Don't worry. It's going to be fine." I spoke quietly.

"Thanks," he smiled nervously.

"Take care. I'll see you tomorrow."

"Sure, Kate. Have a good night."

"You, too, Preacher. Sleep well."

I was the last one in the press box by the time I filed my story, well after midnight. I locked my equipment in a cupboard at the back of the room and took the elevator down to field level.

It was dead quiet in the corridor to the players' exit. Even the cleaners had packed it in for the night. My footsteps clattered hollowly in the stillness. Just past the entrance to the Titan clubhouse I heard another sound. It was just an echo, really, as if someone had dropped something. I walked more quickly.

Then there was another sound, the suggestion of footsteps. I stopped, looking back over my shoulder. No one. I laughed. I was getting spooked.

Suddenly a baseball flew past my head and crashed into the gate at the end of the corridor. Another bounced next to my right ankle. I moved closer to the wall and ran. It was only a few more yards to the exit, but by the time I got there, half a dozen balls had just missed me. Going through the gate, I heard ghostly laughter.

I ran to my car, fumbling in my purse for my keys. Once inside, I locked the doors, turned on the engine, and hit the road, tires squealing. I was having trouble breathing. Once I got to King Street I pulled over until I stopped shaking, then lit a cigarette and pulled back into the road.

I noticed a car behind me, the only her car on the

154

street. I speeded up and ran a red light at Bathurst, then turned north on Spadina and east on Adelaide, narrowly missing a drunk on his way home from his local. There was no sign of the other car. Either I'd lost him or he hadn't been following me in the first place. Probably the latter. I would laugh at myself in the morning. All I wanted to do was get home and pour myself a stiff drink. I only hoped the prowler had left my liquor cabinet alone.

I pulled into the garage and sat for a moment before I got out of the car. Remembering something I'd once read about self-defence, I clutched my keys in my right fist, the points extending between my fingers. Fat lot of good that would be if I was attacked, but it made me feel I was doing something.

I walked quickly up the front steps and was just putting my key in the lock when a shadow on the corner of the porch moved towards me.

"Get back or I'll scream," I shouted. "I have a fierce guard dog inside."

So, it wasn't original. The shadow chuckled.

"Nice try, Kate. Except I already know Elwy."

I stood, frozen with fear, as he moved into the light. It was Andy Munro. I burst into tears.

"Hey, hey, stop that. I didn't mean to frighten you."

He had the panicked look men get when faced with tears. He took the keys out of my hand and unlocked the front door. He put his arm around me and led me inside.

The door to Sally's apartment opened, and a uniformed constable looked out. Andy reassured him and helped me up the stairs.

Elwy was waiting in the living room, meowing indignant questions. Andy took my bag, put it on the coffee table, and let me down onto the couch. Elwy came and sat on my lap.

"You need a drink." Andy went into the kitchen. I

sat snuffling, cuddling Elwy and wishing I'd learned how to cry pretty. I never could figure out how Audrey Hepburn managed it. When I cry, my eyes get puffy and my nose runs. By the time Andy returned, I was calm and, I hoped, not too horrible-looking.

"Do you want to tell me what that was all about? I don't usually have this effect on women."

I hiccupped, trying to laugh.

"I think I let my imagination run a little bit wild. Everyone has been telling me to be careful, you included, and it finally got to me."

I told him about the incident with the baseballs, which seemed to worry him; but by the time I'd described my hair-raising ride through the empty streets of downtown Toronto, we were both giggling.

"You're lucky you didn't get arrested for dangerous driving."

"But I was awesome. Just like James Bond."

That turned him serious again.

"But you're not James Bond. You're Kate Henry. A reporter, not a secret agent. If you go around bursting into tears at the sight of a policeman, what would you have done if it was the murderer, faint?"

"I don't faint, you sexist. I merely cried out of relief. If you had been someone else, I would have . . ."

"Yes?"

"Screamed. And the officer you've got in with Sally and T.C. would have heard me."

"In this case, yes. What if the crazy at the stadium with the baseballs had wanted to do something more than scare you. What then?"

"I can run fast."

"You can outrun a baseball? Ben Johnson can't outrun a baseball."

"I'm in good shape. I could get away."

"Fine. You go on believing that if you want to. But

do me a favour. Don't hang around empty ballparks until this thing's settled. Can't you write your stories somewhere else?"

"I guess." I yawned.

"I'd better go. It's getting late."

"And I've got to clean this place up."

"That can wait. You look exhausted."

"Right. I'll do it in the morning."

"Don't go out until you've talked to me. I'll call at ten. Promise?"

I nodded, yawning again, and walked him to the door.

"Any problem, just shout. I'll speak to Constable Santos before I leave."

We stood awkwardly at the door for a moment. Andy put out his hand. I took it.

"Take care," he said, finally, and left.

"I will," I said, to the closed door.

I was carrying the glasses to the kitchen when there was a soft knock on the door. I went back.

"Who is it?"

"Andy."

I opened the door.

"Um, I came back because I forgot to say what I came over here to say. I wanted to apologize for yelling at you at the stadium. You wouldn't return my call, so I came to say it in person. I shouldn't have yelled at you."

"Apology accepted."

"But I was right, damn it. Wasn't I?"

He started down the stairs before I had a chance to answer, a smug smile on his face. I locked myself in again and picked up Elwy from the couch.

"Come on, my fat friend. I need a cuddle tonight, and you'll have to do."

13

I didn't open my eyes until nine-thirty, when the Elwy
Wake-up Service went into phase two. Phase one
involves sitting on the next pillow, staring at me and
purring loudly. In phase two, he walks around on my
body. If that fails, he nips my ear. I've never slept soundly
enough to experience phase four.

I groaned and cursed a bit, but Elwy was right. It
was time. I looked out the window. Rain.

I went down and knocked on Sally's door, but they'd
already left. The papers were on the bottom step. My
exclusive with Sandi Thorson got good play. Jimmy
Peterson had a piece from the police desk on page one,
too. The other papers didn't have anything for me to
worry about.

I was on my second cup of tea, engrossed in the
crossword puzzle, when the phone rang. It was just ten.
Nice to find a man of his word. I answered in my best
voice, the way I used to do when I was a teenager.

What a waste. It was Tiny Washington.

"We want to talk to you, Kate. Preacher, Gloves, and me. It has to be private."

"Okay. Where do you want to meet?"

"Can we come to your house?"

"Sure, I guess so."

"We'll be there in half an hour."

I had just given him directions and hung up when the phone rang again.

"Good morning, Kate. How are you?"

"Much better, thanks, Andy."

"What are your plans today?"

I crossed my fingers. I wasn't really going to lie.

"I'm not going anywhere for a while. I don't even know if there will be a game tonight if this rain keeps up, but I'll be here until this afternoon, for sure, cleaning up."

"Okay. I'll check with you later. Call me if there are any problems."

"I will. Andy, one question, if you don't mind. Did you find anything in Sultan's safety deposit box?"

"No. Just some contracts and financial papers. It looks like the murderer got whatever it was that Sanchez was using for blackmail. Either that or it was hidden somewhere else entirely. If we could find it, we might have a few new suspects."

"Who do you have on the list so far?"

"Of blackmail victims or suspects?"

"Either, or both."

"We know Kelsey was paying him off, and Thorson. Thorson paid $5,000 a month, Kelsey $2,000. But Sanchez was putting more than $10,000 in the bank each month."

"Try David Sloane. He was seen with Sultan in a bar here. He doesn't drink, he doesn't spend time away from his family in Toronto, and he couldn't stand Sanchez."

"Thanks for the tip. Anything else?"

"No, not really. Except that I don't much like being a target for this guy. Isn't there anything else you can do? Can't you set a trap for him with the glove?"

"Not without putting the child in danger."

"I guess you're right."

"I have someone watching your house in case he tries to come back, but I don't think he will. He was pretty thorough last night."

"Tell me about it," I said, distractedly. I hadn't realized there might be cops around. I thought they were with Sally and T.C. When I hung up I went to the front window. Sure enough, a cruiser was parked up the street. Damn.

I dialled Tiny's number. No answer. It was the same at Joe's. Karin Gardiner told me Gloves had gone out. It was too late to head them off. I'd have to get them inside quickly.

I watched for Tiny's car while cleaning up the living room. When I saw the Cadillac coming down the street I went to the front door and rushed them upstairs into the kitchen.

"I'm sorry about that, but there's a policeman watching the house."

"Oh, man. What have you got us into?" Tiny was upset.

"I tried to call when I realized, but you'd already left. They think the murderer might have broken in here last night."

"That explains the mess," Gloves said. "I thought you were just a bad housekeeper."

"Why are they here, Kate?" Tiny asked.

"I can't tell you right now. Please don't ask."

I poured coffee and sat at the table with them.

"What did you want to see me about?"

"Preacher told me what you were talking about yesterday," Tiny said. "Then I talked to Gloves, and we decided that we should tell you everything we know."

"Why not go to the police?"

"There are things we'd rather not talk to them about," said Gloves, "things that could get some of the players in trouble. That's their business, but it might help find the murderer."

"Go ahead."

"You've treated us fairly as long as I've been with the team. So you can decide what we should do."

"Some of it has to come out eventually, Gloves."

"But you'll keep quiet about it now?"

"I can't write anything until the murderer has been caught unless the police want to release it."

"All right. What do you think is going on here?"

"There are two possibilities. One has to do with the blackmail," I said, looking at Joe Kelsey, "which I know is going on. The other has to do with drugs, which is what I can't really talk about. But there is a drug connection with Sanchez, too. One or the other has to be connected with the murders. Or both."

"Preacher, why don't you tell Kate what you know," Tiny said in a tone of voice that was more an order than a request. Kelsey squirmed, but began.

"There was something I did when I was in the minor leagues that I'm ashamed of. If it came out, my career would be over. I've never told anybody about it."

"We don't want to know," Tiny said.

"Well, last spring, I found an envelope in my locker. It had something in it from that time. Something that got into the papers down in Tennessee. There was a note with it, telling me to come to the batting tunnel early the next morning."

He paused. Tiny and Gloves nodded encouragement at him.

162

"Sultan was there, working in one of the cages. He didn't say anything at first. After I'd been waiting for about five minutes he asked me to help him load the pitching machine. While we were doing it, he said, 'Sure is interesting what you can find in old newspapers.'

"Then he told me that it would cost me two thousand dollars a month to keep quiet."

"So you paid him?"

He shrugged.

"Some guys spend that much on tips. I had the money. It was better than losing my career. But the money wasn't the problem. I hated knowing that he knew. Every month when the payment was due he would look at me a lot when he was talking to people and laugh, just to show me how easy it would be."

"The bastard. Do you know of anyone else?"

"It's not the kind of thing that comes up in conversation, Kate," Gloves said, a bit exasperated.

"I know he was blackmailing Thorson. Sandi told me. And from what you said yesterday, Gloves, maybe David Sloane, too. I tried to ask him about it, but he wasn't saying anything."

"Sloane? What's Sultan have on him? Drinking coffee?" Tiny was incredulous.

"Maybe he was caught exposing himself," I said.

"But you don't seriously think that Sloane did it?" Gloves said, when we'd stopped laughing.

"He has a powerful temper," said Tiny. "But what about Thorson? Why was he killed?"

"The police haven't found the blackmail material yet. It wasn't in Sultan's condo or his safety deposit box, so they think whoever killed him took it. What if Thorson killed Sultan, then tried to blackmail Sloane with the evidence he found?"

"Did Thorson say anything to you, Joe?"

"No."

"Kate, you talked about drugs. What did you mean by that?"

"I'm not supposed to talk about it."

"Come on, Kate. We're trusting you." I decided to follow my instincts.

"Tiny, remember on Saturday, when Sultan gave T.C. his glove?"

"Yeah. He was trying to show me up."

"Whatever. On Monday night, T.C. gave me the glove to fix because one of the laces was coming loose. I found baggies full of cocaine inside the padding. Yesterday was the second time someone broke in here trying to find it."

"Who knew he had it?"

"You were there when Sultan gave it to him, Tiny. I don't know who else saw. But he had it at the ballpark Sunday. Any number of people could have seen it. He was getting autographs."

"I signed that glove on Sunday," Tiny said. "I told him he'd never be able to catch anything with it."

"I did, too," Kelsey said. "I didn't really notice anything about it."

"Me, too," said Gloves.

"Exactly. So did Stinger, Alex, and Mark Griffin. And heaven knows who else noticed it."

"So where does Thorson fit into that one? He was killed Sunday night."

"Damned if I know."

We'd put four brains together and come up with zilch. "Let's forget motive for now," I said. "What about opportunity? Who has keys to the stadium?"

"You mean who could have been there Sunday night? Any of us could have hung around," Gloves said. "And some of us have keys. I got one from Moose one time when I had to go in on an off-day. I never gave it back. It could have been me."

"Or me," Tiny said. "No one has ever worried about keys. Quite a few of the guys have them."

"That doesn't really matter, come to think of it," I said. "The way that clubhouse lock was taped, anyone who bought a ticket to Sunday's game could have hidden in the stadium and got into the clubhouse later."

I was making more coffee when the knock came on the door. I'll rephrase that. I was making more coffee when the irate pounding came on the door. I wasn't surprised when I opened it.

"Staying home this morning to clean up, are you? And you've invited a few friends in to help you, I suppose. They look like they're really handy with a broom."

Staff Sergeant Munro stormed into the kitchen.

"Look. I am the policeman here. I am the one investigating these murders. I don't tell you how to write stories, Kate. I don't tell you guys how to play baseball. Because I'm an amateur at your jobs. Correct?"

"We were just . . ."

"Just what? You have coffee together often, do you? This is a regular occurrence, is it? Do me a favour. Don't treat me like an idiot."

The players had got up from the table as soon as Andy arrived. Now they were trying to sidle inconspicuously out of the door. It would have been funny any other day.

"We'll see you at the ballpark later, Kate," Tiny said.

"Thanks for the coffee," said Gloves.

"Yeah, guys, thanks for dropping in." I wished I could sneak out with them.

When they left, I turned on Andy angrily. The best defence is offence.

"What do you mean by barging in here?"

"What do you mean by lying to me?" He was shouting, too.

"I never lied to you."

"You said you were going to stop playing detective."

"I never did. And besides, I'm not playing detective. If they want to come and talk to me, they can. I didn't *ask* them to come."

"Don't give me that crap."

"Crap?! You want to talk crap?"

We were practically nose to nose, screaming, when the phone rang. I picked it up and barked a hello.

"Kate, it's Moose. Are you all right?"

"I'm just fine," I shouted.

"What's the matter?"

"Nothing. Sorry." I turned my back on Andy and lowered my voice. "What can I do for you?"

"I was just calling to tell you about the memorial service. If it's a bad time you can call me back."

"No, it's fine. When's the service?"

"Tomorrow, at three."

"Where?"

"At the ballpark."

"You've got to be kidding."

"Thorson was Protestant, Sanchez was Catholic. We couldn't hold it in a church. And we needed lots of room."

"Moose, that is really tacky."

"How can you say that? We're going to do a very tasteful service."

"All right, Moose, I'll be there. I wouldn't miss it. But, Moose?"

"Yes?"

"What if it's still raining?"

"It's not supposed to."

"Whatever you say. Who's conducting the service?"

"The Mayor, Father Scanlon, a Spanish-speaking

priest from Our Lady of Perpetual Help, and the Anglican archbishop. Some of the players will speak, too. We haven't got a rabbi lined up yet."

"Moose, you're too much. See you later. You going to get the game in tonight?"

"We're going to try. Get ready for a long night."

"Is there likely to be batting practice?"

"I doubt it."

"Okay, see you later. Thanks for calling."

I hung up the phone and went to the stove.

"Coffee?"

"Please."

I brought the mug to him, avoiding his eyes.

"Sugar's on the table."

"Thanks."

I'm not sure who began to laugh first. Probably me. He looked so contrite.

"Let's start again. How very nice of you to drop by, Staff Sergeant. To what do I owe this unexpected visit?"

"I just happened to be in the neighbourhood."

"Would it insult you if I said you are lying through your teeth?"

"I guess not. I came because I got a call telling me that three suspects had just arrived at your house. Why didn't you tell me they were coming when I talked to you?"

"Who called? The guy across the street?"

"Yes, Constable MacPherson."

"The Boy Scout from the ballpark the other day?"

"The very one."

"Why?"

"To keep an eye on you."

"Is this person going to follow me around? When did you plan to let me know?"

"I was going to tell you when I took you out for lunch."

"When you . . ."

"And that was going to be when I just happened to drop by around lunchtime."

He shrugged. I laughed.

"I give up."

"I'll pick you up at one."

19

Andy took me to Kuri, a Japanese restaurant on the fringes of trend heaven in Yorkville. One of my favourites. The owner greeted us both by name.

"You've been here before?" Andy was surprised.

"What, sports writers aren't supposed to like anything but hot dogs?"

"Come to think of it, not many policemen come here either."

"So you're a misfit in your profession, too. Welcome to the club."

The sushi bar was full, so Kuri led us to a small tatami room and took our orders himself, recommending the toro and hamachi as particularly fine. Andy ordered in Japanese.

"I spent a year in Tokyo in my twenties," he explained.

"What were you doing there?"

"At the time I said I was finding myself."

"And did you?"

"No, but I learned how to order in Japanese."

"Must come in handy."

I was a bit nervous. Was this a date? I decided to stick to business.

"Tell me how Sanchez died."

"Baseball bat, same as Thorson. One swing."

"Like a baseball swing? Or from overhead, like an axe?"

"A level swing to the head. Just over the right ear. He was hit from the front as he came into the bedroom."

"You figure someone was waiting for him?"

"Or hid there when he heard him come in. The bat was one of several Sanchez had in the room. I guess the guy just grabbed whatever was handy."

He popped an ikura sushi, salmon roe wrapped in seaweed, into his mouth and I thought of my grade-school etiquette lesson on dinner-table conversation. "Jane's cat was run over today" was not considered appropriate. I was glad Miss Bushell wasn't at lunch.

I tried to visualize it. If Sanchez had been hit on the right side of his head, the swinger, facing him, had to have been swinging lefthanded.

"Was Thorson also hit on the right side of the head?"

"With Thorson, it wasn't one swing. It looks as if there was more of a struggle. The guy just caught Sanchez by surprise."

"Why a struggle?"

"There were bruises on Thorson's arms and body. We think he got knocked out near the equipment room and was then dragged to the shower room and finished off."

"Could you tell if the attacker was left- or right-handed?"

"Nothing conclusive. The blows seemed to come from all angles. It looked like whoever did it went a bit nuts."

"So the two murders were very different? Are you sure there weren't two murderers?"

"That's still a possibility."

"That's what I was talking with the guys about this morning. Thorson killing Sanchez because of the blackmail, then taking the material he found and trying to blackmail one of the others."

Andy busied himself with a paper-thin ginger slice and smiled.

"Right. It's none of my business."

"It is my business, but I prefer to talk about something more pleasant than murder over lunch."

"If you order us some eel, I promise to talk about anything but murder."

"You've got a touch of blackmail in your soul, too, Kate Henry."

While we ate, I did what I usually do when I'm a bit shy with someone new – I interviewed him.

"The last thing I thought I'd be when I was growing up was a cop, like my father. I didn't see much of him when I was a kid because he was always working, but I worshipped him. I never felt like I could live up to his expectations and I gave up trying when I was about thirteen. I went into serious adolescent rebellion."

"Most kids go through that."

"But most kids get a chance to outgrow it and make peace with their fathers. I never did. He was killed first."

"How old were you when he died?"

"Sixteen. My mother woke me up late one night to take me to the hospital. He'd been shot making an arrest. He was in a coma for three days before he died, so I never got a chance to speak to him again."

He took a sip of tea and looked embarrassed.

"Enough ancient history."

"So you decided then to become a cop. Sorry, policeman."

He smiled.

"I'm a cop. No. I went to Trent University – a general arts course – to see what I wanted to do. I mainly drank beer and tried to get laid and played in a terrible rock band. I dropped out, lived on a commune, hitchhiked around the country. Standard sixties stuff. Then I went to Japan. Do you really want to hear all this?"

"Absolutely."

"I taught English there and fell in love with one of my students. I thought I would stay forever. But that's hard, in Japan. Foreigners can only go so far inside their culture. So I left with a broken heart."

He laughed.

"Anyway, I came back with a stronger sense of who I was and what mattered to me. It was time to settle down. I went back to university, took a criminology course to fill in my schedule, and the rest . . ."

He shrugged.

"History," I said.

"Turns out I was very good at it and I liked it. It must be in the genes. So, within three years I was a cop, within four a husband, within six a father, and within ten, divorced."

He signalled for the bill.

"And that's the end of my tale."

"Or the beginning."

"True."

"And your mother?"

"Alive and well. And remarried."

"Don't tell me."

"Yes, to a cop. What else?"

He drove me to the office, down Yonge Street. I looked at the sleazy storefronts and desperate-looking people and wished I could see it all through his street-wise eyes. He'd probably arrested half of the characters we were passing. I decided that since lunch was over, I could get back to my favourite subject.

"What leads are you following now? Have you checked with bookies? Has anyone made any big bets on the playoffs since the murders? Maybe there's a clue there?"

"We have, but there's nothing big, here or in Las Vegas. The vice-squad guys checked with the local bookies. Some people connected with the team do bet. Bill Ramsay, the trainer, your friend Moose Greer, and a couple of the executives, but it's strictly football and basketball."

"It would have to be. What are you going to do about T.C.? He has to go back to school. Are you going to send a cop along with him?"

"No, he's going to stay out for the rest of the week. His teacher has given him some work to do and I've assigned a constable who is good at helping with homework. She's got kids of her own. We should have an arrest by next week and things can go back to normal."

"You think so?"

"Don't you? You haven't solved the case yet?"

"Well, there are still a few details to fill in."

"You'd better hurry."

"Do you really know?"

"I'm sorry, Miss. I'm not at liberty to reveal that."

"You're just bluffing. If you knew, you'd have arrested him by now."

"Well, there are still a few details to fill in."

"Rat."

Laughing, he pulled up in front of the *Planet* building. "What time do you want to go to the ballpark? Donald MacPherson will pick you up."

"Oh, God, it's going to be so embarrassing being followed around by that guy. He's so officious."

"He's a good cop. He's just young and over-anxious. Be nice to him. He'll get you home when you're through."

"Okay. Have him come at four-thirty. He doesn't have to be in uniform, does he?"

"No one has to know he's a cop. Just say he's a long lost love or something." He snickered at the thought.

"Yeah, sure. Thanks, I guess. And thanks, really, for the lunch. I enjoyed it."

"So did I."

It was still raining at four-thirty, but I decided to go to the ballpark anyway. Anything was better than sitting around talking about the Titans' chances in the playoffs with the armchair managers in the newsroom. The murders were old news. They were back to baseball. Never mind that there was a killer loose out there, probably in a Titan uniform.

Constable MacPherson, champion of ladies in distress, showed up right on time in one of those unmarked cars that no one would drive but a plainclothes cop or a smalltown high school teacher. He wasn't in uniform, but he still looked like a cop.

He was obviously annoyed at being assigned to babysit, but he was a ball fan, which mitigated his humiliation a bit. I was disgustingly nice to him, telling him all the boring inside stuff fans find so intriguing. He'd loosened up a bit by the time we got to the ballpark. I took him in to see Moose.

"You're getting your wish, Moose," I said, after introducing them. "I have someone to take care of me. Maybe you'd better give him a press pass so he can follow me around."

"I'm glad. I just hope he doesn't cramp your style."

"He's not going to follow everywhere, are you, Don?"

"No, ma'am. You can go to the ladies' room alone."

"A sense of humour, yet."

"The guys are going to love it," Moose laughed.

"Can we try to be a bit subtle about this?"

"Of course, Kate. I won't tell a soul. Do you want the weather report?"

"Not really."

"It's going to clear up at seven."

"And rain again at seven-thirty, right?"

"No. It's going to rain again at eight."

"Terrific. Just time to get it started."

"And there's a front going through at nine-thirty that will clear it all up."

"Times like this, I wish I was paid by the hour. See you later. Come on, Constable."

There was nothing doing in the clubhouse so I took my shadow to the empty dugout. We sat on the bench and watched the rain.

"I can't count the hours I've spent sitting in dugouts waiting for the rain to stop. It's kind of peaceful."

"It's kind of boring, too."

Doc Dudley came from the clubhouse with a towel wrapped around his neck, the ends tucked into his jacket. He went out onto the field and ran lonely laps in the drizzle, working off his nerves. Max Perkins, the Detroit starter, joined him half a lap behind. The two ran in step, but separately, in silence.

"Strange way to have fun," said Gloves, sitting next to me on the bench.

"Why are pitchers so weird?"

"Beats me," he said, glancing curiously at my escort. I introduced them.

"Constable, would it be all right if I had a word with Gloves privately? We'll just be over there where you can see us."

"In the rain?" Gloves protested.

"Just for a minute," I said, leading him towards the bullpen. He grabbed a towel from the bench and put it over his head.

"I'm sorry about this morning," I said.

"You are in some deep shit with that guy."

"He thinks I'm invading his turf."

"The way he was carrying on, maybe you'd better stop."

"I got it straightened out. I've got a job to do, too."

"Are you really trying to find the murderer?"

"Why not? It would be a great story."

"Well, I've been doing some thinking about what we were talking about this morning."

"So have I. I'm just more confused."

"The drug thing. We were interrupted before we could talk about it this morning. I can't think of anyone who would be crazy enough to try to import drugs. There's always plenty around for the guys who want it. One of the shoe reps has a source. He's in and out of the clubhouse all the time."

"Maybe he set it up."

"He's just small time. He gets guys grass or women or porn tapes, whatever they want. But he only deals coke in grams."

"Grams aren't enough for anyone who's seriously into coke, Gloves. Who are the guys who are using heavily?"

"Nobody I know."

"Would you know? Could you tell?"

"I have known guys who were heavy into it, like Terry Jackson, and none of the guys here now act that way."

Jackson was a pitcher who had been traded to Texas the previous season.

"Jackson? Are you kidding?"

"You didn't know that?" Gloves laughed and started back towards the dugout. "Keep at it, kid. But be careful."

I was getting sick of all this touching concern. I was

sicker of it by game time after being followed "discreetly" by Constable Donny, inconspicuous as a giraffe. The other writers were born journalists, every one, and I gritted my teeth through a lot of teasing.

After dinner I took him out into the hall.

"No offence, but there really isn't room for you in the press box. Stay here in the hall with Charlie. He's in charge of security on this floor, and he'll tell you if anyone isn't supposed to be here."

"Sure, I'll take care of him," Charlie said. "You come along with me, Constable. I was in the force myself for twenty-five years."

I liked the thought of MacPherson enduring good old Charlie's stories for a whole game. With a rain delay expected at that. He glared at me as I left. I smiled.

"Be sure and show him where he can watch the game, Charlie."

Charlie, already in mid-reminiscence, waved.

I almost danced to my seat. Moose gave me the game notes. Alex Jones had a seven-game hit streak (big deal); Stinger Swain was celebrating his thirty-fourth birthday (thirty-four, going on thirteen); Mark Griffin hadn't given up an earned run in nine innings; and Mitch Saxon, the Tigers' backup catcher, wouldn't be available because he had "pulled his groin." (Keep it up and you'll go blind, kid.) Invaluable stuff.

It was a terrible night for a ballgame, damp and chilly. All the players were wearing thick woollen sleeves under their uniform jerseys, except for Swain, who always has bare arms, even when it's snowing. He thinks he looks manly. I think he looks like a jerk, but what do I know?

It would probably be a sloppy night. Batted balls are unpredictable on wet artificial turf. Some speed up when they bounce, rocketing through the infield, giving even the best fielders no chance. Some get trapped in puddles, leaving the outfielders poised like idiots ten feet back.

Nothing happened until the top of the fifth, when Rafe Morgan, the Tiger third baseman, hit a homer to right, driving in two guys who had reached base on a walk and an error to Owl Wise.

In the bottom of the inning the rain got heavier and lightning flashed out over the lake. The outfielders looked nervous.

"Why don't they call the damn thing?" I asked.

"If they get the rest of the inning in, it's an official game," Moose said.

"Thank you, Moose. I can always count on you to explain the finer points of the game."

"You're getting testy, Hank. Maybe I should call your babysitter."

"Put a sock in it."

Red O'Brien obviously wanted to avoid the loss if he could. With the soggy fans shouting approval he trudged out of the dugout towards home plate. As he got within talking range, lightning flashed, followed by a tremendous clap of thunder. Red shrugged his shoulders and pointed to the sky, as if to say, "See, even He agrees with me," and the umpire broke up.

"Call it, call it," chanted the crowd.

The four umpires huddled at home plate with O'Brien and Billy Saunders, the Tiger manager. After a few seconds the crew chief stepped back and waved his arms, delaying the game. The crowd cheered.

"Cards, Kate?" As usual, Stan Chapman was looking for a fourth for bridge.

"Not tonight, Stan."

I had come prepared with the latest Martha Grimes mystery in my briefcase. I put my feet up on a chair and escaped into the English countryside until the game resumed at 10:45.

The rest was anticlimax. The Titans couldn't put together enough hits to score, and the game ended at midnight, 3–0 for the Tigers.

"Oh, goody. Now we get to go chat with the cheery chaps downstairs. What jolly fun."

Cheery they weren't. But with the pennant won, there was none of the gloom that had become habitual after losses. I grabbed a few philosophical quotes from the ones who were talking, and left. Game stories weren't really big news any more.

My faithful bodyguard was waiting for me in the corridor. He fell in step beside me on the way to the elevator.

"Enjoy the game, Constable?"

"Not much. What's it like in there after they lose?"

"You don't want to know. Your illusions would be shattered."

"How come?"

"They all pretend they care about the team, but they're really thinking about their own numbers and how good they'll look come contract-renewal time. But they'll get the Tigers tomorrow."

"I hope so. I just want to see them beat the Yankees. Those are the guys I can't stand."

"And with any luck, you'll still be stuck with this lousy assignment and you can see the games."

He looked at me sheepishly.

"Hey, if I were in your shoes I'd feel the same way. And I appreciate your discretion tonight. Thanks."

I invited him into the deserted press box while I filed my story. Then he drove me home, full of questions about my glamorous job. He walked me to the door, like a prom date, and asked when I'd need him in the morning.

"Get a good night's sleep. I won't be going out until the afternoon. I'll call Staff Sergeant Munro and tell him."

He waited until I'd unlocked the door, then made sure there weren't any villains lurking in the hallway before he left.

I locked up and poured myself a glass of wine. Then I went to my study, Elwy racing me up the stairs, and turned on the TV. We watched a Perry Mason rerun. Elwy is particularly fond of Raymond Burr.

20

The sun backlit Father Michael Scanlon's full head of white hair, making a halo, and didn't he know it as he beseeched the Lord to take Sultan Sanchez and Steve Thorson to His heavenly bosom. The phoney old priest's list of their virtues sounded more like a scouting report than a eulogy. He had been chosen for the service not for his position in the religious community – his was an insignificant suburban parish – but because he was a charter member of the Titan booster club. He said grace at all the Player of the Month luncheons.

It was a glorious day, the sky a deep autumn blue and the air Indian summer warm. The mourners, at least ten thousand of them, filled the seats between the bases behind home plate. The players, their families, Titan personnel, league officials, and local bigwigs were in folding chairs on the field. The widows were veiled in black, sitting together near the visitors' dugout.

The priest stood on a crêpe-draped dais behind the mound, praying into a microphone. His amplified voice was out of sync with his lips. A small plane flew over the stadium, trailing a banner that read "Pedro Sanchez, Steven Thorson, Rest In Peace." At game time, the same plane would be advertising the appearance at a local strip club of Miss Nude Northern Ontario.

"I'm surprised they didn't bring in Ernie Banks for the service," I muttered to Jeff Glebe.

"How come?"

"It's a beautiful day. Let's bury two."

Father Scanlon was the last of four ecumenical speakers, following Father Jorge Guerrero, who had spoken in Spanish for fifteen minutes. It looked as if Scanlon was out to break Guerrero's record, but he finally wound down and left the stage, stopping to embrace Sandi Thorson as the cameras clicked.

Tiny Washington and David Sloane took his place. Tiny looked embarrassed, Sloane composed.

"I knew Sultan Sanchez for thirteen years," Tiny said, too close to the microphone, which squealed. "I played with him and I played against him. He always played hard. He was a leader on every team he was with. He taught pride to the young players. He also helped us remember to enjoy what we did. No matter what was going on, Sultan could make us smile.

"Steve Thorson was a competitor. He played with intensity and never gave less than 100 per cent whenever he was on the mound. He was the heart of this team. He made us play our best because winning was all that mattered to him. He was respected by every hitter in the league.

"You all loved them, too, so I guess you know what all of us guys on the team are feeling. We will do the best we can to honour their memory, but we will miss them, on and off the field."

There was scattered applause, quickly shushed, from some fans who forgot where they were. Then Sloane stepped to the microphone.

182

"Let us pray," he began, and heads bowed around the infield, a ragged collective movement.

"It's a prayer Wave," I whispered. Glebe shushed me.

Sloane shut his eyes and raised his arms to the sky.

"Lord. You have taken two of our brothers from us. You know why You had to do it. It is not our place to ask why. Thy will be done. They are not truly gone because they live on in all of us.

"We stand before You not in sorrow, not to weep, but to thank You for letting them be with us for a time, for enriching our lives.

"We knew them well. We knew Pedro Sanchez and Steven Thorson as teammates. We knew them in joy and in sorrow. We knew them as brothers. We were soldiers together in a daily battle. And we will not shirk the battle because they have left us.

"Lord, we dedicate ourselves to finish what our brothers helped us begin. And we will dedicate our victory to them. We will prevail. We will triumph over our foes and become World Champions and dedicate our championship to their memories."

"Yeah, but where are they going to send the World Series rings," whispered Jeff. I fought back a giggle and Sloane, incredibly, began to sing.

"Mine eyes have seen the glory of the coming of the Lord!"

Ten thousand voices joined his as the airplane banked over right field.

"And here I was hoping for 'Onward Christian Shortstops,'" I said.

"It always happens at funerals," I explained to Jeff on the way to the reception. "Even real ones. My dad's a minister, so I've been to a lot of them. I always get the giggles."

"You cry at weddings, I take it."

"And in movies, at hockey games, tractor pulls, and shopping centre openings. It's only funerals that make me laugh."

"This one would have made a corpse laugh," Jeff said. "I wonder what Father Guerrero said?"

"Probably that Sultan's giving 110 per cent in heaven."

The reception, which was private, was in the Batter's Box, the bar and banquet area of the stadium. The lineup snaked down a concrete stairwell that smelled faintly of hot dogs, popcorn, and beer. Everyone looked a bit odd dressed in their Sunday best. Just as we came to a bend in the staircase, Sam Craven tapped me on the shoulder.

"I was hoping I would see you," he said. "It's a terrible business, isn't it? That was a nice piece you did on Sandi. I'm sure she appreciated it."

"Thanks, Sam." I introduced Jeff. "When did you get in from New York?"

"Just now. I've been getting Steve's affairs wound up. Talking to insurance agents, things like that. Tragic business."

"Who gets the money?" Jeff asked.

"Most of it goes to Sandi. His parents inherit some, too. I had a small policy on his life, of course, as did the Titans. But they'll have to pay the remainder of his contract to his estate."

"Would they have had a policy on Sanchez, too?"

"I would imagine so."

We had made it to the Batter's Box. I let Craven go in first. I wanted to watch him go through the receiving line. Ted Ferguson faked it, shaking his hand warmly, but passed him on quickly to Father Scanlon and turned his attention to us.

"Kate. Jeff." He nodded, then took my hand in both

of his. "Thank you so much for coming. What did you think of David's comments? Very moving, I thought."

"Indeed," I said. "Very inspirational."

There was a small commotion just ahead of me. As Craven leaned to embrace Sandi Thorson, she twisted out of his arms.

"I can take care of myself," she hissed at him. "You just take your cut and leave me alone."

Craven glanced quickly around to see if the exchange had been overheard, then smiled and moved on. It was my turn.

"Are you all right?"

"Just stand here for a minute, would you?"

"Of course."

"I hate that man so much. Why did he have to come?"

"It would have looked funny if he didn't, Sandi. He was Steve's agent, after all."

"He's horrible."

Surprised at her vehemence, I changed the subject.

"Will you be leaving Toronto now?"

"I'm flying to California tonight. The funeral is tomorrow."

"What about Stevie?"

"He went home with my parents last night. I didn't think he should have to go through this."

"I think you're right."

"It's hard enough for me. I don't know what I'm going to do, but I've got my mom and dad. They'll help."

"And you have lots of friends."

"Baseball friends. They forget pretty quickly. There will be a new pitcher. And a new wife. But some will stay friends, I hope."

I started to move on, but she stopped me.

"I wanted to thank you for the article you wrote yesterday. My parents thought it was real nice."

"You're welcome. Take care of yourself. Let me know where you end up. I'd like to keep in touch."

"I will," she said, then suddenly, clumsily, embraced me, embarrassing us both a little.

Sultan's wife Dolores, whom I had never met, was lovely. Tiny and dark, she had extraordinary eyes and a great deal of style. Her English was not very good, but her teenaged son Eduardo helped interpret. He was tall and handsome, very like his father. The Titans had signed him to a minor-league contract early in the season. They each shook my hand formally.

I declined coffee and cookies and went up to the press box. The ground crew had dismantled the dais and taken up the chairs and were rolling the batting cage into position. A few Tigers were waiting for early batting practice.

There was no one else around but the technicians setting up for that night's broadcast. It was very peaceful. The players on the field were horsing around in the sunshine. Life goes on. Many of the mourners who had just left the park would be back in a couple of hours, dressed in jeans and Titan sweat shirts, eating hot dogs and drinking beer. The voices that had sung hymns would be screaming at the umpires.

In this philosophical mood it didn't take long to write my piece on the memorial service. The team provided transcripts of the speeches. I even managed to quote David Sloane without mocking.

When I finished, I rested my head on my arms.

"Sleeping on the job?"

It was Moose's voice, and his strong hands massaging my neck and shoulders.

"That's heaven. Never stop." I felt like Elwy. If only I could purr. "You may be saving a life here, Moose. I'll do what I can to get you the Order of Canada."

He laughed and dug his knuckles into the really sore part between my shoulder blades. I groaned.

"Time's up. I've got work to do," he said, giving me a last hearty thump.

"Maybe it'll be a short one tonight."

"I wouldn't bet the rent on it."

21

The game wasn't short, but it was so much fun that no one cared. A day that had started in tears and sombre reflection ended in jubilation. The Titans were winning 14–3 and still at bat in the bottom of the eighth when Jeff Glebe leaned over to check on a fine point of sportswriting.

"Does this qualify as a trouncing?"

"Not yet. You need a twelve-run lead for a trouncing."

"A drubbing?"

"Yeah, you only need ten for a drubbing."

Every Titan had at least one hit. Tiny Washington, David Sloane, Joe Kelsey, and even Alex Jones had hit home runs. Kelsey also had a triple and a single. He was due up next, with two out, and looking for a double, if Wise got on base.

The count was full, but Owl fouled off pitches to stay alive. He finally tapped a single between first and second. The crowd was excited, aware how close Kelsey was to hitting for the cycle: a single, double, triple, and home run in the same game. He would be the first Titan ever to do it.

He hit the first pitch hard to left field. It looked like a home run, but hooked foul at the last moment. There was relieved laughter from the fans. They wanted the double.

He gave it to them on the second pitch, a ball hit solidly into the gap in left centre. The fans stood and applauded for so long that Kelsey was forced to tip his cap, embarrassed. Dummy Doran signalled for the left fielder to give him the ball and pocketed it to give to Preacher.

The cheering finally stopped and the game resumed. No one was disappointed when Tiny Washington grounded out to end the inning. And when the Tigers went down in order in the ninth I even had half an hour left to my first deadline.

Downstairs in the clubhouse it was as if a spell had been broken. The memorial service had closed a door. The mourning was over. And the one-sided win had put the fun back in the game.

"Bring on the A's!" shouted Costello, wearing a towel and waving a beer in the air. It was hard to hear him over the music booming from the tape deck in his locker. Bruce Springsteen.

"Turn it down, Bony," I yelled. "I can't hear you."

"Bring on the playoffs! The season's over!"

He was right. It was his last start.

"Not too shabby – twenty-three wins! That's a two and a three. Two-enty the-ree. Whee hee!"

He'd drawn a small crowd of reporters, all laughing at his antics. He downed his beer and danced to the cooler to get another. He came back with three and jumped up on his stool.

"I'm going to party tonight," he said. "But first, I will accept questions from the media."

He turned down the music, but it didn't make much difference, there was so much yelling going on around us.

"You want to know the secret of my success? Food! All my career they've been telling me to lose weight. This year I just ate. Burgers. Fries. Ice cream. Pizza. Spaghetti. Lasagna. Manicotti. Canelloni! Gnocchi! And vino! Gallons of vino!"

His accent grew Italian as he talked, and he began to wave his arms around. By the end of his list, he was almost operatic.

"Eating to excess is the secret of my success!"

His teammates burst into applause. He bowed deeply, then turned his back and bowed again, dropping his towel.

There was no point asking a serious question. I went in search of more sensible folk.

Joe Kelsey was sitting in front of his locker, a huge smile on his face. He shook his head as I approached him.

"He shouldn't have done that in front of you," he said.

"I've seen a naked bum before, Preacher. Don't worry about it. It's his big day."

"It's the kind of year you dream about."

"What about you? Hitting for the cycle isn't exactly an average day at the office."

"It's just a fluke, you know. You just get lucky one day. Not like twenty-three wins. Now, that's truly something. He was blessed this year."

"And it couldn't have happened to a nicer guy. Do you think he'll stop being so gloomy?"

Kelsey's smile broke out again.

"Bony? Are you kidding? He wouldn't be happy if he wasn't unhappy!"

We both laughed.

"What did you think about at the plate during the last at bat?"

"To tell you the truth, I was worried I wouldn't even get the chance. Then Owl got that seeing-eye hit and I felt like it was meant to be. I've never felt so relaxed at the plate."

"And then you almost blew it by hitting a home run."

"Yeah, I was praying for it to go foul!" He stopped suddenly. "Don't put that in the paper. I don't really pray for things like that."

"I know. What about the service today? Did it help get the team back together?"

"I think it did. We put the tragedy behind us. Now we just have to win it for them."

"Think you will?"

"I don't see why not. But that's not the important thing."

"What's more important?"

"Finding the man who killed Sultan and Steve. And making sure he can't get anyone else."

"Of course. Sorry. It's just hard to remember that here tonight."

"We don't mean any disrespect, Kate."

"I know."

Constable Donny was waiting for me outside the clubhouse, so excited by the game that he couldn't shut up, even in the press box while I was writing. The story, under the circumstances, wrote itself, and we were out of there by midnight.

"What are your feelings about drinking on duty, Don?"

"I shouldn't, why?"

"We've got time to hit last call at the Fillet of Soul. Do you mind?"

"I'd like that. I've never been there."

"Let's just call it semi-duty, then."

"You're the boss."

He was grinning.

The bar was crowded. We found a table in the corner and the constable unbent enough to have a beer.

"One won't hurt," he said

"I promise I won't let you drive drunk, okay?"

Sarah brought our drinks. I introduced her to my companion, with no explanation. She'd go nuts trying to figure out what kind of cradle-robbing I was into. It would do her good.

Like most fans, the constable had strong opinions about what was right and wrong with the team and its management. It was good to listen to him. We sometimes forget who we're writing for. But when our second round arrived, I changed the subject.

"How long have you been on the force?"

"Almost three years."

"Are you assigned to homicide?"

"No. This is my first time."

"Are you enjoying it?"

"Well, I wish I was more involved in the case."

"Have you worked with Staff Sergeant Munro before?"

"No. I've just heard about him."

"What have you heard?" Subtle, Kate, subtle.

"That he's tough. That you'd better not screw up. He's hard to work for, but he's the best."

"He has a bit of a temper, doesn't he?"

"I've never seen him really mad, but I've heard it's something."

"I know."

MacPherson shot me a sly look and smiled.

"He chewed you out pretty good, didn't he?"

"How do you know?"

"I saw him when he got there. He was steaming."

"No secrets, eh?"

"I shouldn't have said anything."

"On the contrary. I love gossip. What else do you hear about Munro? What about his personal life?"

"He doesn't have much, they say. He was married, but his wife left him. Since then, he's been a real loner. Too bad, he's pretty good looking, for an older guy."

I winced. He noticed.

"I don't mean old. It's just that . . ."

"How ancient is he? In his forties?"

"Oh, no. He's not that old."

"Well, I'm glad. I'd hate to think he'd have to retire before he solved these murders."

"I think I've said something wrong."

"Not at all. I used to think forty was old, too. I changed my mind my last birthday."

"Oh, gee. I thought you were a lot younger."

"Thank you, Donald. Maybe it's time to take this old bag home. It's way past my bedtime."

He apologized all the way there, and walked me to my door again.

"Miss Henry, you won't mention to Staff Sergeant Munro that we were talking about him, will you? I was out of line."

"I'm just old, Constable, not stupid. It will be our secret."

"Thanks. Good night."

I didn't notice the parcel at first. I was greeting Elwy and setting down my things. It was a large manila envelope with the rest of my mail on a small table just inside my door. Sally had left a note with it.

"This was waiting when I got home at six. It's not ticking."

It might as well have been. A sheaf of papers was held together with a paper clip. On top was a clipping from a paper in Nashville, Tennessee, dated in June, 1982. It was the report on a raid of a homosexual bath

194

house. Listed among the found-ins was one Kelsey, Joseph Baines.

"Oh, God. Poor Preacher."

The second page was a photocopy of a confidential memorandum from the security chief of the Southwestern Inter-Collegiate Baseball Association. It stated that during the 1973 season, a number of players from Oak Park College in Texas had thrown games for a pay-off. As the offenders had graduated, the report suggested that no action be taken. The first name on the list was Steve Thorson.

"I don't really want to know this," I told Elwy.

The third document was a photocopy of a year-old police incident report filed in Toronto. It described an assault by David Sloane against the persons of Marie Sloane, Merlin Sloane, and David Sloane, Junior. The final notation, following a pedantic description of the incident, was that the charges had been dropped by Mrs. Sloane.

"That sanctimonious bastard!"

Elwy's response was to roll over on his back for a stomach scratch.

"And what am I supposed to do with this?"

He warbled an interrogatory half-purr, half-meow.

I drew myself a hot bath. A half-hour soak later, I wasn't sure what I had learned, except some pretty juicy answers to a few questions. All I knew was that things didn't look too good for one David Sloane. Or Joe Kelsey, for that matter. But who had sent the parcel? And why?

22

In the cold sober light of day it became obvious that I had to call Andy Munro. He came right over, showing his gratitude in the oddest way.

"When did you get this?" he shouted.

"Last night, late. It was here when I got home."

"Where was that idiot MacPherson?"

"He'd already left. And he's not an idiot. I didn't even see it until I'd been home for five minutes."

"And you opened it. Just like that. You didn't think to call me first, of course."

"How did I know what was in it? I would have felt like a prize dope if it had been a letter from my mother and I got you out of bed at one o'clock in the morning."

"What were you doing out so late?"

"What's it to you?"

"When was the game over?"

I decided not to tell him about luring his constable from the straight and narrow.

"I had a story to write. Do you mind?"

"Don't you ever, ever, pull a stunt like this again."

197

He'd stopped shouting, but he was spacing his words ominously, in a coldly controlled voice.

"Now I'm going to take this material to the lab, even though the chances of getting any useful fingerprints are nil now that you've pawed over them. And you're coming with me so I can get your fingerprints for comparison."

"But . . ."

"NO BUTS. I've had it with your meddling. You're coming with me. NOW."

I took a deep breath and tried to keep my voice calm.

"Look, Staff Sergeant Munro. You can't just go around yelling at civilians. It's police harassment. Or something. Badgering a witness. I called you. I gave you the stuff. Now leave me alone. I've got work to do. If you want my fingerprints, you can tell Constable Donny to get them tonight at the ballpark. I will not be ordered about by you."

"Constable Donny?" Munro did a slow take, then cracked up. "You call him Constable Donny?"

"Not to his face."

"It's perfect."

"Well, he is a bit earnest."

"Earnest? He's an escapee from *Leave It To Beaver*."

"Except he's too young to have heard of it."

"He's too young to have heard of the Beatles!"

"Paul McCartney's old band, right?"

I guess we weren't mad any more.

"All right," Andy said. "You win. You don't have to come with me. But don't go out. Whoever sent this to you might try to contact you. And don't tell anybody else about this."

"Scout's honour."

"Do you think you can get through the rest of the day without meddling?"

"I'll try, sir."

"I'll send Constable Donny to pick you up. Try not to get the boy into any trouble."

The phone rang. I waved him out the door.

"Nice game story," said Jake Watson. "And the piece on the funeral was fine. Was it as bizarre as it sounded?"

"More. What do you want from me today?"

"I need some stuff for the playoff supplement on Monday. Position-by-position comparisons of the two teams. And a sidebar on what's happening with the betting odds. Can you call that contact of yours in Vegas?"

"Good idea. I'll see if I can find him."

I had done a story several years back about sports betting and dug it out of my files. The guy I had used wasn't one of the big names, but he was well connected and very helpful. Jerry something. Bergman. Jerry Bergman. His number was in one of my books. It took a while but, luckily, he hadn't moved.

"The odds have been wild on the American League," he said. "Up and down like the proverbial toilet seat."

"That's not surprising."

"No, but it's a headache for the books."

"I guess. How's it gone?"

"We don't set the line until the two divisions are clinched, so that was Sunday for the American League. As soon as the Titans won, we posted the odds at 7–8 for the Titans."

"Those are pretty good odds, aren't they?"

"Yeah. The Titans are better, plus they beat the A's eight games to four this season. But that was before Thorson got killed."

"One man makes that much difference?"

"Sure. Assuming they go to the three-man rotation for the playoffs, he pitches three times in the seven-game series."

"I see what you mean."

"So when he got croaked, the money started coming

in for the A's. What's happening about that, anyway? Anyone been arrested?''

"Nothing. The players seem to have bounced back.''

"Never saw a ballplayer who would let a little thing like grief get between him and money on the line.''

"You got it. So what happened to the odds?''

"Well, some money came in on the A's Monday, but when the odds shifted, people began betting on the Titans again. But the action's been soft. I mean, who cares, right? Not like when the Yankees or Dodgers are involved. Then we get a lot of tourist money coming in.''

"You don't get a lot of people calling up from Oakland or Toronto making bets?''

"We don't do phone bets.''

"Really? You've got to be there?''

"Strictly cash and carry.''

"I thought people bet on the phone all the time.''

"Only local bookies carry accounts. There are guys here who act as agents for gamblers around the country, but they're putting cash down at a shop.''

"Hunh. Could you run it down for me day by day?''

"Okay. Sunday, it was 7–8, Titans. Monday, after the murder, it dropped to even money, and that's a big drop out here. Tuesday and Wednesday, the same. Thursday, we started getting more Titan action and by today it's back to 6–7 Titans.''

"Okay. Let's pretend I'm really stupid, here, which won't be hard. What do these numbers mean? If I bet $100 on the Titans today, and they win the playoffs, what do I get?''

"You're going at it backwards. I'll tell you what you'd have to bet to win the $100. All the lines are based on five dollars. You put up more money to bet on a favourite. At 6–7, you bet seven dollars to win five. If you're betting on the A's, you bet five to win six. In other words, if you wanted to win $100 on the Titans today, you'd have to bet $140."

"So I'd end up with $240."

"Exactly."

"And on Sunday?"

"At those odds, you had to put up $160 to make your $100."

"And why did you change the odds?"

"Thorson's death, mainly."

"But you didn't change them after Sanchez died?"

"The line hadn't been set at that point. We probably set them a bit lower than we might have because of Sanchez, but a player doesn't make as much difference as a pitcher. Like in football. A defensive end getting injured doesn't affect the odds the way it does when a quarterback goes down."

"I'm stupid again. Why does the money coming in make a difference?"

"Because bookies aren't in the business to lose money."

"I'm not that stupid. But how does it work?"

"The ideal situation for a bookie is when he has as much money bet on one team as on the other. Then the losers pay off the winners, and the book collects his percentage from everyone.

"But if more money is bet on one side than the other, we have to compensate. That's where the odds come in. They are set to reflect what we think the action will be. In this case, we assumed that more people would want to bet on the Titans. So the odds make the Titans a little less attractive and encourage betting on the A's."

"So if a lot of people bet one way, the odds shift."

"Right."

"If just one person makes a big bet?"

"Same thing, if the bet's big enough."

"Do people bet big money on the playoffs?"

"Most of it's just small stuff, but I've had three or four in five figures this week. One shop took a ten-grand bet on the A's Sunday just after the odds were posted. Nice timing."

"Be nice to have that kind of money to play with, wouldn't it?"

"Out here, that doesn't even raise an eyebrow. I've got customers who win and lose that much every day. They're nuts, of course, but they put food on my table. Who am I to judge?"

"Listen, thanks a lot, Jerry. I appreciate it."

"You bet."

I wondered if estate lawyers say "will do" a lot.

I was fixing lunch when the penny dropped.

What if that bet wasn't just lucky timing. What if someone had inside information? Like that the ace of the Titan staff wouldn't be in the playoffs. I called Jerry back.

"This guy who bet ten thousand on the A's. Do you know who he is?"

"He didn't come here. He's a regular at a little place over on South First Street. A buddy of mine works there. Why?"

I explained my theory.

"Could be. I'll see what I can find out."

"Could you find out the time he placed the bet, too? Thorson was killed sometime after seven forty-five."

"Check."

I called Bergman back a couple of hours later.

"No luck. The guy who took the bet doesn't get in until later. Where are you going to be tonight?"

I gave him the number of my press box phone and left for the ballpark.

23

There wasn't a whole lot to do before the game, for a change. With the pennant clinched, there was no particular need to talk to the Yankees, which suited me just fine. It was a pleasure to be able to treat them as also-rans.

I spent some time with my favourite New York beat writer, Arnie Shapiro. He was a funny little guy from a daily in New Jersey who managed to cover the Yankees without becoming self-important, a rare feat.

He had delicious gossip. One of the outfielders had picked up a woman in a Cleveland bar who turned out to be a transsexual who hadn't quite finished her/his surgery. The manager had got into a fist fight with his bullpen coach on the plane. And the team bus had been chased by a gang of Detroit thugs after a relief pitcher pissed out the window on their car. An average road trip for the princes in pinstripes.

They weren't all jerks, mind you. Just most of them. I spent a pleasant ten minutes talking with Gene Ridell, their shortstop. He had his family with him and wanted advice on sightseeing. A friendly man, he was stunningly rare in his interest in people and places outside of the game. He was also a good person to interview about playoffs. He'd been in a lot of them. It might make an interesting sidebar.

"Are you very disappointed in losing the division?"

He shrugged.

"I've been there before. I'll be there again."

"What about the pressure? Everyone predicts that the Titans are going to blow it because they haven't been in the playoffs before."

"Well, by the time you get to the playoffs you've already been through a lot of weird stuff. The playoffs are just a little weirder. They'll do fine if they don't psych themselves out of it."

"What's the hardest thing to deal with?"

"I guess the feeling that in the playoffs everything you do matters so much. Baseball should be peaceful. There should be room for mistakes. Errors are part of the game. Failure's part of the game. But it's hard to remember that when there's so much on the line. The playoffs and World Series turn baseball into a very unforgiving game."

"So your advice to the Titans would be?"

"Relax. Try to enjoy it. This is what it's all about. And don't forget what brought you here. Teamwork. No one wins a game all by himself. If you strike out, that just means it's someone else's turn to drive in the run. You'll be asked to do other things that you'll do well. Don't dwell on your failures."

"Easier said than done."

"For sure. I was a basket case my first time. You're talking to the guy whose error cost us a game in the playoffs three years ago. But I also drove in the winning run in the next game."

"Which do you remember more?"

"Winning felt better, but I'll never forget the error. I guess I just cancelled myself out. I might as well not have played."

"You're pretty philosophical today."

"You get that way when you know you're going to be watching the World Series on television."

"I guess. Have fun with your family here. And have a good winter, if I don't see you before you leave."

"You too. And, hey. Watch out for that pressure!"

"Thanks. I'll just write one game at a time."

The last series of the season is like the last week of school, with the same schizophrenic blend of relief and anticipatory nostalgia. The world is about to change abruptly. Most of the people you see every day will be gone. And not all of them will be back. It's great to get away from the schoolyard bullies and teacher's pets, but you know that in a month you'll be missing them. Of course, I still had to get through the playoffs and World Series, even if the Titans didn't go that far. A lot of column inches to fill. I went to the press box to write.

The game was pretty uneventful. There were so many backup players and minor-leaguers in the lineup it looked like spring training. Harry Belcher started in what would have been Steve Thorson's spot. Since he had spent the season in the minors on merit, no one expected him to do much; but he pitched a pretty good six innings before Red brought in his relievers to get some work. Titans lost, 6–5.

The biggest excitement in the press box was when Arnie Shapiro called his office in New Jersey and found out that Hank Chambers and Jim Wilder, former Yankee stars, had just been arrested.

"What for? Drunk driving?"

"No way. Possession of cocaine and dangerous weapons."

"Ouch."

I'd met both players one spring when they'd come to the Titan camp to see Moose. I turned to him.

"Are you okay?"

He was pale. "It's a shock. Those guys are friends of mine."

"Have you seen them recently? Did you know they were into this kind of stuff?"

"No, I haven't. I didn't. Stupid bastards. What were they messing with that shit for? Damn."

He sent one of the press box runners to check the sports wire. The kid came back in ten minutes with a scrap of paper torn from the machine. Moose read it and passed it to me. It was an early story, just reporting that the pair had been arrested, along with three others, in a police drug raid. I passed it to Arnie.

"That's tough, Moose. I'm sorry."

"That stuff just brings you grief."

After the game, I stopped by Gloves Gardiner's locker and told him about Chambers and Wilder.

"Doesn't surprise me," he said. "They're maniacs. I thought they were strung out when I saw them last week."

"Where?"

"At Yankee Stadium. Didn't you see them? They were there before the game Thursday night. They had seats right next to our dugout."

"Huh. I guess I didn't recognize them."

"I think that's the day you got there late."

That late lunch, haunting me again.

"It's too bad, anyway. They used to be fine players."

"But not particularly fine people," Gloves said.

"They had it all once. Now it's drugs and guns?"

"And greed, same as most people. The most Chambers ever made in his career, even when he was a batting champion, was probably $150,000. Kids two weeks out of the minors get that these days. Maybe he figured the world owed it to him."

"So he was bitter."

"Wouldn't you be?"

"Since writers don't make that kind of money, I don't think the temptation will be laid in my path."

"And you're probably a better person for it."

"Thanks, but I think I'd be willing to face the challenge."

MacPherson drove me home in silence. Something was wrong, but I was too tired to ask. When we got to my house, he spoke, looking embarrassed.

"Did you tell Staff Sergeant Munro about last night?"

"Lord, no. Why?"

"He was acting real funny today. I looked up one time and he was standing there laughing at me. For no reason."

"I can't imagine what that could be about."

"I don't think it was anything I said or did."

"I'm sure it wasn't."

I realized I hadn't heard from Andy since I'd given him the blackmail material. Both Joe Kelsey and David Sloane had been at the stadium but I hadn't spoken to either of them. I thought of calling Andy, but it was almost midnight. He might get the wrong idea. He might be right.

Besides, I had a day game to cover. I went to bed and dreamed I was on deadline, trying to find a phone in Yankee Stadium to file my story. But they were all being used by people who wouldn't get off: Steve Thorson, Joe Kelsey, Gloves Gardiner, David Sloane, Sam Craven, Jim Wilder, Andy Munro, Moose Greer, Jeff Glebe, even Sally. When I tried to tell them I needed the phone, they didn't hear me. I shouted. They laughed. I went down a corridor, into another room. A shadowy figure came at me with a bat. I couldn't move. I tried to scream and woke myself up in a sweat. Elwy was on my chest, sound asleep.

24

I was still groggy and grumpy when Andy called the next morning. He didn't have much news.

"We're still checking. Both Kelsey and Sloane have some sort of alibi for at least one of the murders. Sloane was home both Saturday and Sunday night. Kelsey was out with Eddie Carter after ten on Saturday and with Carter and his wife on Sunday until nine."

"Thorson was already dead by then, wasn't he?"

"Probably."

"He must have got to the stadium around seven-thirty, according to Sandi. I can't see him hanging around for long. He was in a hurry to get to the cottage."

"Exactly."

"Sloane's only alibi is his family?"

"But they're firm on it."

"He probably threatened to beat them up again."

"Kate, just because you don't like somebody doesn't mean he's a murderer."

"One, we know he's a violent man. Two, he bats lefthanded."

"And three, he had no motive for Thorson."

"Maybe Thorson knew something. Maybe he saw Sloane coming out of Sultan's place."

"He just happened to be passing by?"

"Why not?"

"Then what?"

"What do you mean?"

"How did Sloane happen to be at the ballpark?"

"He followed him?"

"You're reaching, Kate."

"I guess."

"Right. Other than that, what's your day look like?"

"Nothing much. It's a day game."

"And you're going to be in tonight?"

"Probably. Ted Ferguson's throwing his annual bash for the team and local bigwigs but my invitation seems to be held up in the mail again."

"Okay. Constable Donny will meet you at the ballpark."

At least I was able to drive my own car there. A small blessing.

I was busy before the game. Beat writers from around the league had deserted their teams to come and get an early start on their playoff coverage. So there were lots of questions to be answered about new players and the status of the murder story. I was getting more attention than the players.

Moose stopped me on my way to the press box.

"Are you busy tonight, Kate?"

"As it happens I have a rare free evening. Why?"

"Do you want to come to the party tonight? I owe you one after my behaviour on Sunday."

"Sure, where's the party?"

"At the Hilton. But I'll pick you up. Say about seven? Dinner's at eight."

"Gee, just like a real date. Do I get a wrist corsage?"

"Don't push your luck. I'll see you at seven."

"Come at a quarter to. We'll have a drink first."

I left the field early. There were a couple of scouts I hadn't been able to reach the day before. I tracked them down and got the last few quotes I needed for the playoff supplement. They thought that even without Thorson and Sanchez the Titans were a sure bet to go to the World Series.

Which reminded me — I hadn't heard back from Jerry Bergman. I phoned, but he wasn't in. His office promised that he would get back to me.

It was a loose afternoon, on the field and in the press box. The fans were whooping it up, carrying banners through the stands and heckling the Yankees. Most of the reporters were relaxing, drinking beer and speculating on the winners of the league Most Valuable Player and Cy Young awards.

"Thorson could get it," I said. "He didn't win as many games as Costello, but his e.r.a. was lower and he had more strikeouts. Besides, being dead gets the sympathy vote."

It was generally agreed that there was no likely MVP candidate on the Titans. Three or four guys were having career years, but there wasn't a standout who had carried the team.

Rookie of the year was another matter. Alex Jones got everybody's vote in the press box. It was hard to see how the other writers in the league could overlook him.

He made a case for himself in the top of the first inning when he went deep into the hole behind third base and threw out a runner with a perfect, seemingly impossible, throw. That won him his first standing ovation of the day. A bases-loaded triple into the left-centre-field gap in the bottom of the inning won him the second. They would have given him a standing ovation for picking his nose. It was that kind of afternoon.

Red let each of his regulars play two or three innings, then sat them down, but even the subs were hitting. Flakey Patterson shut the Yankees out for seven innings. He would be starting the second game of the playoffs, and looked ready to go. Red sent Goober Grabowski to start the eighth, but the fans called Patterson out of the dugout for another ovation. Final score was 8–1, Titans.

I was home by six, with just enough time to shower and change before Moose came. I wore a dress Sally had talked me into buying. It was cut high in the front and low in the back, with sequins on the bodice and a short tight skirt slit halfway to my bum. Moose was even tall enough for me to wear my spike heels without looking like a giant. I was finishing on my makeup when Jerry Bergman called.

"Sorry I took so long," he said. "My buddy who took the bet was out of town yesterday. First of all, the bet came in at seven. That's a bit early."

"Seven your time. What are you, two hours earlier?"

"What time is it there?"

"Almost six-thirty."

"It's twenty-five after three here. Three hours."

"Hmm. Who made it?"

"A guy they call the Hawk. Strictly a small-time guy. The guy at Leroy's figures it was someone else's money."

"They don't know his name?"

"Jimmy Hawkins, I think. He's a rounder. Played some pro ball about twenty years ago. I doubt if he made it to the big leagues for more than a cup of coffee. But he boasts about it when he's boozing, which is most of the time."

"What does he do?"

"Drives cab, when he's working. Mainly he chases that one big score. It looks like he's found it."

"How would he have that kind of money?"

"Like my buddy said, maybe it wasn't his."

"Okay. Thanks a lot for your help. I'll let you know if anything comes of it."

"Any time."

My *Baseball Encyclopedia* was worth a look. If he'd played at all in the major leagues they'd have his year-by-year records.

Hawkins, James Bonner, didn't take up much room. He'd amassed a total of fifty-four major-league at bats, spread over three years, with the Seattle Pilots and Milwaukee Brewers, when the team moved. It looked as if he'd made a few trips up in September before he was dropped. I checked his birth date: September 13th, 1947, in Vulture Gulch, Arizona.

Vulture Gulch — "hard by Rooster Creek." I flipped back through the book. Same home town, same minor-league system. Close enough in age to make no difference. I felt sick.

The phone was answered on the second ring.

"Constable MacPherson speaking."

"It's Kate Henry. I have to speak to Staff Sergeant Munro. It's urgent."

"He's not here."

"Find him."

The doorbell rang downstairs.

"Tell him to get his ass over here as fast as he can. I think I'm in a lot of trouble."

Moose rang again.

"Is that your doorbell?"

"Find Munro and get here *now*."

25

I ran down the stairs and opened the door with what I hoped was a casual smile.

"Sorry, Moose. My zipper got caught. Didn't mean to keep you waiting."

"No problem," he said. "You look terrific. Are you ready to go?"

"Just about. I thought we were going to have a drink."

He came in.

"Martini? I've got the glasses in the freezer."

"Martini's fine," he said, following me to the kitchen.

"So, what's tonight going to be like? This is my first time at the big event."

"No big deal. A lot of community types to be nice to. But there's usually a suite later where the players can go and get shit-faced."

"You can hardly blame them this year," I said, getting the gin out of the refrigerator, trying not to check the clock too obviously. "It's really fun to be around them these days. I must admit I never thought I'd still be around when they won their first pennant."

"I had some doubts myself."

"Are all the credentials ready? You've been so busy I've hardly seen you in days." I added a few drops of vermouth and started an olive hunt in the cupboard.

"They came from the printers this afternoon. The girls will be stuffing the envelopes tomorrow."

"When can we pick them up?"

"Monday, at the hotel. The media rooms open at noon."

"Here you go. I hope it's to your liking."

We carried our drinks into the living room. I excused myself and went to the bedroom, stalling. I came back fastening earrings, then sat down and raised my glass to him, straining to hear the sound of a car. I hoped they wouldn't use sirens.

"To the Titans getting into the World Series."

"To the Titans."

I tried not to gulp my drink. Five more minutes passed in stupid chatter about playoff arrangements. Then he drained his glass.

"I guess we'd better get going."

"We've got time for another. I need more fortification before facing that crowd." I jumped up and took his glass. "I'll be back in a jiffy."

Where were they? I mixed the drinks slowly and was just starting to pour them when Moose came into the kitchen.

"You know, don't you?"

"Know what?" My voice didn't sound natural even to me.

"How did you figure it out? You have figured it out, haven't you? That's why you're acting so strange."

He began to walk towards me.

"Listen, Moose. I don't know anything. I don't know what you're talking about. Honest. Look, maybe we'd better get going. I don't need another drink."

He leaned against the counter with his arms folded across his chest.

"I didn't mean to, you know. I never meant to kill Sultan. I just wanted to knock him out." His voice was flat, unemotional.

"You were looking for the glove."

"I didn't know he'd given it away."

"You got the drugs from Chambers and Wilder in New York."

"I needed the money. Gambling. I was going to sell the drugs to get the loan sharks off my back. When the coke disappeared, I had to find another way. I read the papers that Sultan had, and when Steve came to the stadium Sunday night, I tried to get him to throw the playoffs. He wouldn't do it – I had to kill him. He knew I'd killed Sultan because I knew about the blackmail."

"And you got your old friend Hawkins to make the bet for you in Las Vegas."

"It was my only chance," he said, starting to pace around the small kitchen. "Why did you have to keep on? I tried to warn you. I tried to scare you off. I don't want to hurt you. You're my friend. Why didn't you stop?"

"You sent me the blackmail files to make me think it was Sloane or Kelsey."

He took a carving knife from the rack over the counter. "But it didn't work."

"You don't want to do this. I won't tell anyone."

I backed away. He followed me. I used the only weapon I had. I threw the martinis in his face, then the heavy crystal pitcher, and ran.

I was almost at the door when he caught up. He grabbed me from behind, by the hair.

I heard feet pounding up the stairs and screamed. The door burst open. Andy was the first one in, followed closely by MacPherson, guns drawn.

"Don't do it, Greer."

I could feel the point of the knife at my throat. Moose had my arms pinned behind me with the other hand.

"Take it easy," Andy said. "Let her go."

"Get out of here," Moose screamed. "Just get the fuck out."

Andy started to move towards us, his free hand stretched out in front of him. I heard a growl. It was Elwy, on the back of the couch, his fur standing on end.

"Just relax, Greer." Andy's voice was very calm. "Drop the knife. We won't shoot you unless you hurt her."

"No. Stay back."

Moose took the knife from my throat and gestured towards them. With a yowl, Elwy launched himself through the air. Moose looked towards him. I bent my leg and raked the spike heel down his shin and into his instep. I wrenched free while he was off balance. I could hear my dress tearing as I rolled out of reach.

He started after me. MacPherson dove across the room and tackled him. Andy held the gun on Moose while MacPherson cuffed his hands behind his back.

Moose began to cry. MacPherson, panting, read him his rights.

"Are you all right?" Andy was kneeling next to me on the floor.

"I'm fine," I said, but my voice wasn't. "I'm a bit shaky. I'll be all right."

He helped me to my feet, then sat me on the couch and went to use the kitchen phone. Elwy climbed onto my lap and purred. In a few moments, I heard sirens screaming down the street. They choked into silence outside my front door and Andy's partner ran up the stairs, followed by two more officers. Along with Constable MacPherson, they hustled Moose towards the door.

Before they left, Moose turned to me.

"I'm sorry. I didn't want to hurt you, but you wouldn't stop."

"I'm sorry, too, Moose."

The door closed behind them. Andy came and sat next to me. He took my hand.

"You've got some guts, Kate. Do you feel up to coming to the station and making a statement?"

"I can't. I've got a story to write."

"Goddamn it, woman. The story can wait."

"Just let me phone the office and tell them I'll be filing. Where are they taking him?"

I told the astonished night editor to hold some space for me, then called Jake Watson at home.

"I'll write the main story, but if you want anything else, send someone down to the Hilton. There's a team party going on. They'll all be there. Someone will have to get the news to Ferguson. Problem is, he hasn't got a p.r. man to handle it any more."

By the time I got back from the phone, Sally and T.C. were with Andy. They crossed the room to hug me.

"Looks like I'd better put on the kettle," Sally said.

Over a pot of tea, we began to piece together the story.

"You're going to have to help me on some of the details, Andy."

"If you'll tell me how you figured it out."

"It was the blackmail material that put me on the wrong track at first," I said. "It was such compelling stuff that it took my attention away from the drugs. That's what it was all about. Sanchez and his blackmail had nothing to do with it.

"The drugs were smuggled in on the last road trip from New York. Whoever did it had to know the equipment isn't checked crossing the border. He also had to

219

know that Sultan rarely used his glove and wouldn't notice if it felt different than usual. So it was a safe hiding place."

"Then Sultan gave me his glove," said T.C., his eyes huge behind his glasses.

"But Moose didn't know it until Monday, when I mentioned it to him. He hadn't been able to find it on Saturday in the clubhouse, so he went to Sultan's apartment and broke in.

"I think Sultan came in while he was looking. He grabbed a bat and hit him, just trying to knock him out. When he realized he was dead, he searched the place and messed it up to look like a burglary. He also found the blackmail material.

"I even saw it Sunday night. He was trying to put it away when I brought him home. I didn't notice at the time."

"Why did he kill Thorson?" Sally asked.

"He was looking for the glove in the equipment room when Thorson came in for his fishing stuff. I think Moose just panicked. He needed money. When he lost the dope, he needed the money even more.

"He told me tonight that he tried to use the blackmail material to force Thorson to throw the games he was scheduled to pitch. Thorson refused, but realized that the only way Moose could know he'd thrown games in the past was if he had murdered Sanchez. Once he knew that, he had to die. How am I doing so far, Staff Sergeant?"

"Sounds good to me. Where did he get the dope?"

"That's what started me thinking. Two former players were arrested on drug and weapons charges in New York last night. They're friends of Moose's, but he said he hadn't seen them for years. Then Gloves Gardiner told me that they'd been at the stadium before a game last week. I wondered why Moose had lied.

"That's probably when they made the switch. Moose often used Sultan's glove to play catch. It would be the easiest thing in the world for his buddies, who had the drug connections, to replace Sultan's with the one full of drugs."

"What tipped you?"

"That was a fluke. When I was talking to a bookie in Las Vegas about the odds for the playoffs, he mentioned a guy had bet ten thousand dollars on the A's on Sunday night. That's not so big a bet, evidently, but the timing was odd. Thorson's body wasn't found until Monday morning. So I thought there might be a connection with someone here.

"Just before Moose arrived tonight, the guy from Vegas called me and told me the name of the bettor. He also told me that he had played professional baseball. So I looked him up in the *Baseball Encyclopedia*, found he came from the same little town as Moose, and everything fell into place. That's when I called you."

Elwy jumped up on my lap and butted his head against my chest.

"Right, Elwy, and then you saved my life."

Andy snorted. "An attack cat."

"Elwy is not your ordinary cat."

I shooed them all out and wrote my story. I finished by midnight, despite calls from several other reporters. I politely refused comment, telling them to buy the *Planet* the next morning. Then I took the phone off the hook and took a long, hot bath.

At one I was in my bathrobe on the living-room couch listening to music and sipping a Scotch. Elwy was on my feet. I was about to turn in when I heard footsteps on the stairs, followed by a soft knock. I went to the door.

"Who is it?"

"Special delivery for Detective Kate Henry."

Andy had champagne in one hand, flowers in the other, and a smile on his face.

"Feel like celebrating your first crime solved?"

Elwy rubbed against his ankles and purred.